Noah asked, "Does your skin sting?"

"Not much. The col—

His serious gray eyes searched Kate's face, and then, even more gently, he touched the tip of his forefinger to the tip of hers. "How's that?"

"Fine."

He did the same to the next finger. "How about now?"

"It's okay," she whispered breathlessly. "Thank you."

For a moment there she wondered if Noah was actually flirting—if he was going to kiss her fingers. She imagined his lips lingering on the palm of her hand and him running kisses up her arm, like the hero of an old-fashioned romance.

What had happened to her common sense? Last time she'd made a fool of herself over Noah it had taken her years to recover. It was pointless to expect anything but friendship. Romance was the last thing on his mind. He was still getting over his divorce, and he had a daughter to worry about.

As soon as these cattle were safely delivered, he would thank Kate for her help, then expect her to retire gracefully and discreetly out of his life. On the first plane back to England. FICTION

Dear Reader,

Isn't it exciting that Harlequin is celebrating its sixtieth anniversary? I think it's amazing that this company began publishing romances just after World War II and is still producing wonderful, feel-good stories for contemporary readers all these years later.

As a reader, I've spent many, many happy hours lost between the pages of a Harlequin novel, and as a writer, I consider these books to be the luckiest discovery of my life. What a fabulous job I have, to spend my days weaving my favorite kinds of stories and to share them with readers all over the world.

I'm truly honored to be a part of this publishing tradition, and I'm thrilled that it's exactly ten years since my first book, *Outback Wife and Mother,* was published by Harlequin Romance®.

This latest book, *Her Cattleman Boss,* is also set in the Australian Outback. Along with a passionate romance, it highlights the almost dying tradition of cattle droving. I do hope you enjoy it.

Warmest wishes,

Barbara

BARBARA HANNAY
Her Cattleman Boss

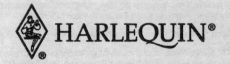

TORONTO • NEW YORK • LONDON
AMSTERDAM • PARIS • SYDNEY • HAMBURG
STOCKHOLM • ATHENS • TOKYO • MILAN • MADRID
PRAGUE • WARSAW • BUDAPEST • AUCKLAND

Recycling programs
for this product may
not exist in your area.

ISBN-13: 978-0-373-17575-8
ISBN-10:   0-373-17575-2

HER CATTLEMAN BOSS

First North American Publication 2009.

www.eHarlequin.com

Printed in U.S.A.

Barbara Hannay was born in Sydney, educated in Brisbane and has spent most of her adult life living in tropical North Queensland, where she and her husband have raised four children. While she has enjoyed many happy times camping and canoeing in the bush, she also delights in an urban lifestyle—chamber music, contemporary dance, movies and dining out. An English teacher, she has always loved writing, and now, by having her stories published, she is living her most cherished fantasy. Visit her Web site at www.barbarahannay.com.

This fall Barbara Hannay brings you
a new Harlequin Romance® duet
Baby Steps to Marriage…

Share the joy of pregnancy,
proposals & parenthood in
Expecting Miracle Twins
September 2009

The Bridesmaid's Baby
October 2009

Harlequin Romance® is delighted to bring
you another fantastic story from
RITA® Award-winning Australian author

Barbara Hannay

*Barbara brings you a sparkling story
that's brimming with emotional insight
and romantic sparks!*

Praise for the author:

"Barbara Hannay's name on the cover
is a sure-fire guarantee of a good read."
—*CataRomance.com*

"Barbara Hannay [delivers] very layered
and life-like characters and a premise that is
overflowing with deep, emotional issues."
—*Romantic Times BOOKreviews*

CHAPTER ONE

KATE Brodie stood with her suitcase beside her, her sensible jacket folded over her arm, and looked across the stretch of sunburned grass to the site of her first and worst heartbreak.

She had hoped to feel calmer about coming back to the Australian Outback after nine years, but her first glimpse of the low, sprawling homestead baking beneath the harsh sun sent her stomach churning like a tumble dryer.

Such an annoying reaction after all this time. She was no longer the naïve English teenager who'd come to her uncle's cattle property for a holiday. She'd recovered years ago from the embarrassing crush she'd wasted on Noah Carmody, her uncle's handsome young stockman.

Kate looked again at the silent homestead with its ripple-iron roof, reaching low like a shady hat over deep verandas, and her throat tightened painfully. She could almost picture her Uncle Angus standing at the top of the front steps, waiting to welcome her, his silver hair shining in the sun's dazzle and his smile as wide as his open arms.

He'd lived in virtual exile in Australia—which had always seemed like the bottom of the world to Kate—

but he'd been her only male relative and she'd loved knowing that he was *there*, like a deep-sea anchor. It was so hard to accept that he'd gone for ever.

Turning slowly, she looked about her, taking in the vastness, the overwhelming emptiness of the Outback. The tourist coach that had brought her from Cunnamulla had already disappeared into the shimmering heat haze and flat, red earth dotted with grey clumps of dried grass stretched as far as the eye could see.

Her uncle's letters had hinted at the prolonged drought in this part of Australia, but she was shocked to see how desperately hot and dry it was.

Nine years ago, these same parched paddocks had been oceans of lush grass, and the creeks had run with clear, fresh water. Pretty green lawns and bright flower-filled gardens had surrounded the homestead.

Now, with the gardens gone, every blade of grass shrivelled, and the earth sun-bleached and bone-hard, the homestead had lost its grandeur. It looked sad and faded, as if it, too, had succumbed to the cruelty of the withering sun.

Four lone frangipani trees had survived the drought and they stood, two on either side of the front steps, like maids of honour. They were ablaze with extravagant blooms, and their gaudy splashes of colour were like thick daubs in an oil painting—pristine white, sharp lemon, deep rosy-pink and rich apricot.

A photographer's dream.

But now wasn't the time for photographs...

A hot wind gusted, picking up gritty dust and throwing it in Kate's face. She ducked her head and blinked hard. After her tediously long journey, dirt in her eyes was almost too much. She was weary to the bone. Jet lagged.

And she still had to face up to Noah.

Which shouldn't be a problem. She was sure Noah Carmody had long forgotten the awkwardness of her teenage infatuation. For heaven's sake, it had all happened when she was seventeen. Noah had recognised her crush, had taken pity on her and kissed her.

Unfortunately, she'd responded with a wantonness that had shocked him. That was the embarrassing part Kate fervently hoped Noah had forgotten.

She'd been so wild and headstrong back then, so desperately in love with him. And with the buoyancy of youth she'd bounced back from his rejection. Focusing on the kiss rather than the rejection, she'd gone home to England with her head full of dreams of leaving school, of getting a job, and saving hard to return to Australia.

She'd planned to work as a jillaroo in the Outback, to meet up with Noah again, and she'd been sure that, given time, she could win his heart and marry him.

Fool.

How pathetic she'd been, fighting her mother's protests and refusing to get her A levels, or to go to university. She'd given up everything for that one dream. And then, at about the same time she'd earned the money to buy her plane ticket to Australia, word had arrived via Uncle Angus that Noah had married an Australian girl.

Even now, all these years later, the memory of that letter made Kate's throat close over. Thank God she'd eventually recovered. It had taken years, but at last Kate was *normal*. Her latest boyfriend, Derek Jenkins, was a rising star in London banking and Kate was quietly confident that she was over Noah. Completely and permanently *over* him.

When she saw him again, she would be as reserved

and polite as he'd always been with her, and the only emotion she would show would be her grief over Angus's passing.

Now Kate marched resolutely across the final stretch of dirt to the front steps, where an elderly cattle-dog, sleeping beneath the low veranda, lifted his head and blinked hazel eyes at her. He rose stiffly and approached her, his blue-and-white-flecked tail wagging.

Kate stopped. She hadn't had much experience of large dogs, and she expected him to bark, but he remained utterly silent, watching her keenly.

'Is anyone home?' she asked.

The dog gave another lazy wag of his tail, and then retreated to the shade beneath the floorboards, like a pensioner allowed to enjoy the shade after a lifetime of hard work.

Kate couldn't blame him for keeping out of the sun. Already she could feel it stinging the back of her neck. Sweat trickled into the V of her bra and made her skin itch. She hurried up the short flight of timber steps into the welcome shade on the homestead veranda.

And stopped dead.

The very man she'd been fretting over was sprawled in a canvas chair. Shirtless.

Kate gulped. And stared.

His face was covered by a broad-brimmed akubra, but she couldn't mistake that long, rangy body and those impossibly wide shoulders. His bare chest was bronzed and broad, and it rose and fell rhythmically.

By contrast, Kate's breathing went haywire.

It was the shock, she told herself, the shock of finding Noah Carmody asleep at midday. The last, the very last thing she'd expected.

She'd invaded his privacy, but, heaven help her, she couldn't stop staring.

She took another step and the veranda's bare floor-boards creaked, but Noah didn't move. Her gaze fixed on his hands, large, long fingered, suntanned and beautiful, loosely folded over the belt buckle of his jeans.

Carefully, she set her suitcase down and continued to stare. His hips were lean, his thighs strong, and his blue-jeans-clad legs seemed to stretch endlessly in front of him. He'd removed one riding boot and kicked it aside, and his right foot now looked strangely exposed and intimate in a navy blue sock with a hole in the big toe. No doubt he'd fallen asleep in this chair before he'd got the other boot off.

'Noah?'

Kate's lips formed the word, but no sound came out. She sent another hasty glance beyond the veranda, to the wide expanse of dry, empty plains spreading to infinity in every direction. She'd get no help from out there.

The house was silent, too. The front door was slightly ajar, offering a hint of a darkened and cool interior, but no sounds came from inside. Beside the door, an old hat with a battered crown hung on a row of pegs, and next to it a horse's bridle and a leather belt with a pocket-knife pouch. The possibility that her Uncle Angus had left them there, planning to use them again, burned a lump in Kate's throat.

She took another careful step towards the door. Someone must be awake—Noah's wife, or a house-keeper at least. But if she knocked she might disturb Noah. To Kate's dismay, her confidence shrank to zilch at the thought of that tall, muscle-packed, bare-chested man waking and setting his cool grey eyes on her.

She could avoid waking him if she went round to the back door. Then she would find the housekeeper in the kitchen. It was almost midday, for heaven's sake, and someone should be up and about. No doubt that someone should wake Noah...

Turning carefully, she began to tiptoe, retracing her steps over the creaking veranda floorboards to the steps. Halfway across the veranda, she heard a deep, gravelly voice.

'Kate?'

She spun around.

It was just as she'd feared.

Noah was out of his chair, standing tall. So tall. And heart-stoppingly attractive with a day's growth of dark beard shadowing his jaw. His eyes narrowed against the sun's glare. 'It is you, Kate, isn't it?'

'Yes.' Little more than a squeak emerged from her tight throat. 'Hello.' She swallowed awkwardly. 'Hello, Noah.'

'Yes. Of course it's you.' His teeth flashed white in his suntanned face as he grinned. 'No one else has that colour hair.'

He crossed the veranda swiftly, and Kate thought, for a pulse-raising moment, that he was going to hug her. Her mind galloped, and with alarming ease she prepared herself for being hauled into his arms.

His bare chest would be warm and solid, and his satin-smooth skin would be stretched over muscles that were whipcord-hard after so many years of working in the Outback. Those amazing, strong arms would be about her once more. So sexy. And comforting, too, after her long and exhausting journey.

But Noah didn't hug her. *Of course*. She should have known he'd be careful and distant.

He held out his hand and shook hers formally. 'This is a surprise—a *nice* surprise—Kate. I'm afraid I—I've been in a bit of a mess since Angus's death. But it's good to see you.'

'You too.'

Shadows lingered beneath his eyes and his cheekbones seemed more prominent than they'd been nine years ago.

She said, 'I was terribly shocked to hear about Uncle Angus.'

Noah shoved his hands deep in the pockets of his jeans. 'It was so sudden.'

His light grey eyes assessed her, taking in her too-fair skin and her travel-rumpled clothes, her pale-red hair, already limp after little more than an hour in the Outback's heat.

He lowered his glance to take in his own shirtless state and his mouth tilted sideways in an apologetic smile. Turning quickly, he snagged his shirt—faded blue cotton—from the back of the chair and he shrugged it on, his big shoulders straining its seams.

Covertly, Kate watched the fluid, deft movement of his fingers as he closed the buttons. Starting from the bottom, inch by inch, like a striptease in reverse, his hunky brown torso disappeared beneath the thin fabric. She hoped she didn't sigh, but she couldn't be sure.

Noah sat down again to pull on his abandoned boot. 'As you can see, I wasn't expecting you. I'm sorry. I'm afraid the wake went rather late last night.'

'The wake?' Kate frowned in puzzlement.

'We held a wake for Angus in the Blue Heeler pub in Jindabilla. A huge crowd came. People from all over the Channel Country.' Noah's eyes lightened momentarily. 'We gave him a great send off.'

'But—but—' Kate couldn't hold back the tremor in her voice. 'But you don't usually have a wake *before* the funeral, do you?'

At first Noah didn't respond.

His mouth pulled in at the corners and his bright gaze narrowed. 'No, not usually.' His voice was cautious and quiet, and his hand came up to scratch the side of his neck. 'Hell,' he whispered.

'What? What's the matter?'

He looked pained and rubbed at the side of his forehead, and she wondered if he had a headache. A hangover?

'You've come for the funeral.' He spoke softly, without looking at her, almost as if he was talking to himself.

'Well, yes. Of course that's why I've come.'

He almost winced as his gaze met hers. 'I'm sorry Kate. I'm afraid the funeral was yesterday. Yesterday afternoon.'

She stared at him in disbelief.

His Adam's apple rippled as he swallowed.

Spinning away from him, she clutched blindly at the veranda railing. Her mouth trembled and tears stung, then spilled. How could this have happened? She'd come all this way!

'Why—?' She swiped at her cheeks, pressed three fingers against her lips as she struggled for composure. Took a breath. 'Why didn't you wait for me?' she asked, without daring to look at Noah.

'I'm so sorry,' he said again and his voice was exceedingly gentle. 'We didn't— I didn't know you were coming.'

'But I said I'd come.' She glared at him. 'I telephoned. I spoke to someone here. I told her I was delayed, but I said I was definitely coming.'

She bit down on her lip to hold back a sob. Noah had

no idea how deeply she'd always loved her uncle. And he couldn't possibly understand that she'd sacrificed an important photographic assignment to come all this way at such short notice. Or that she'd come despite her mother's bewildering indifference to her brother's death.

When Kate had announced that she would attend Angus's funeral, her mother had been predictably surprised, almost offended. *'Darling, no one down there will expect you.'*

But Kate was used to her family's antipathy to their Australian relatives and had learned to ignore it.

Her boyfriend, by contrast, had been disconcertingly eager. *'Of course you must go. Stay as long as you like and have a holiday.'* Not a word about missing her. Until she'd asked. And then, of course, Derek had told her she'd be missed enormously.

So, despite mild misgivings, Kate had been determined to come. It was very important to make a showing of family solidarity. She'd wanted, more than anything, to demonstrate to this tight-knit Outback community that at least someone among Angus Harrington's distant family cared, *really* cared, about his passing.

And she'd wanted the comfort of ritual, of a church service and a kindly minister saying prayers. Without that, she felt as if she couldn't really say goodbye.

But now… She'd flown all this way, had travelled more than ten thousand tedious miles—in a jet, then a tiny inland plane no bigger than a bird, and then finally in a bouncing bus over narrow and bumpy Outback roads—for nothing.

Nothing.

Fighting her gathering exhaustion and despair, she turned to Noah, her voice rising on a querulous note. 'I spoke to a woman. I thought she was your housekeeper. I can't believe she didn't tell you I was coming.'

A muscle worked in Noah's jaw. Frowning, he shook his head. 'You can't have spoken to Ellen. She's been in such a state since Angus died, I sent her into town to stay with her sister.'

Kate huffed angrily. 'Well, I don't know who it was then. I was on my mobile and the line kept cutting out, but I told her that I was held up at Heathrow. We had terrible snow and high winds all over England, and there were twenty-four-hour delays at every airport.'

Sighing heavily, Noah stood with his hands sunk on his hips, not meeting Kate's gaze but looking somewhere out beyond, to the faded sky that hung listlessly above the parched brown paddocks.

'Truly, I'm very sorry, Kate. I didn't get your message. I—I think you must have spoken to Liane.'

'Your wife?'

'My ex-wife. She came back for the funeral.'

'Ex?'

'We were divorced just before Christmas.'

Kate struggled to breathe. Not an easy task when a string of explosions was detonating inside her. She felt as if she was tumbling through the air in slow motion. Noah was no longer married and her world had turned upside down.

In the awkward silence Noah said again, 'I'm really sorry about the funeral, Kate.'

The defeated tone in his voice surprised her. He offered no further explanation. It was almost as if he expected that his former wife would have neglected to pass on an important message. Kate had no choice but to accept that she'd missed the funeral. It was a *fait accompli*.

But she'd come such a long way.

Noah picked up her suitcase and said in the quiet, laconic drawl of the Australian Outback, 'You'd better come inside and I'll brew up a cuppa.'

Kate forced a small smile. 'I think I could really do with some tea.'

With a gentlemanly sweep of his arm, he motioned for her to enter the house ahead of him. They went down a long passage which, she remembered, cut straight through the middle of the house to the big kitchen at the back.

'I'll put your things in this spare room,' he said, ducking into a bedroom that opened off to the right.

'Are you the only person here?'

'At the moment, yes. Ellen will be back soon.'

'Is it all right for me to stay here tonight?'

'Sure.' He shot her a puzzled glance. 'Don't look so worried, Kate. No one expects you to jump on the next plane back to England.'

'I couldn't face that.'

'This room's yours, for as long as you need it.'

'Thanks.' She looked about her, amazed by how familiar the little bedroom felt. She was sure she recognised the single bed with old-fashioned brass ends and white candlewick spread.

Faded pink curtains hung over French doors that opened onto a side veranda. A very old, silky oak wardrobe with an oval mirror stood against the far wall. Looking about her, Kate was sure it was the room she'd slept in when she'd been here all those years ago.

Yes... She recognised the photo of her grandfather hanging on the wall. With his shock of white hair, thick white moustache and erect posture, and seated in a cane peacock-chair on the homestead veranda with his

faithful dog at his feet, he looked like a throwback to
the British Raj.

She remembered the emotional storms she'd weath-
ered during the summer she'd spent here, how she'd
hovered on the veranda, hoping to catch sight of Noah.
The blissful heights and savage depths of youthful
passion and unrequited love. The *embarrassment*. A
shiver rustled through her. She hoped Noah didn't notice.

With her suitcase stowed, they continued on down
the passage to the kitchen.

This room hadn't changed either, Kate decided as she
looked about her at the huge black stove set in a galvanized-
iron recess, and the big scrubbed-pine table dominating
the room's centre. A crumpled green-and-white-striped
tea towel had been flung carelessly over the back of one
of the mismatched chairs, and a clutter of kitchen utensils
dangled from hooks above the stove.

On the far wall a row of shutters had been pushed
wide open to catch the slightest hint of breeze. Everything was unpretentious and homely, just as she remembered, and she found this strangely unsettling. It was
like stepping back in time.

Noah put the kettle on the stove and lit the gas
beneath it. 'I have to go into town this afternoon for the
reading of the will,' he said.

'That's OK. I'll be fine here.'

'You should come too.'

She'd given absolutely no thought to legal matters,
but she was sure her uncle's will would be very straight-
forward. Angus Harrington had been a bachelor, and
she'd always understood that he'd planned to leave this
property to Noah.

Noah had been born here on Radnor station. His

father, Joe Carmody, had been head stockman, but there'd been a tragic accident—a light-plane crash in which both Noah's parents had been killed. Uncle Angus had taken the boy into his home and, although he had never adopted Noah formally, he'd raised him as his own son.

Kate watched Noah now as he moved with familiar ease about the kitchen, fetching mugs and a brown china teapot and yellow sugarbowl.

He looked as at home in this kitchen as he had when she'd seen him working outdoors, or riding a stockhorse. He belonged here, and she couldn't imagine him living anywhere else.

As he set the mugs and sugar bowl on the table, she said, 'I can't see why I need to go to the solicitor's.'

'You're Angus's blood relative. You should be there.'

'My mother might be Uncle Angus's sister, but she's spent her entire life ignoring him.'

Noah simply shrugged. The kettle came to the boil and he turned to the stove to attend to it. Kate watched him pour boiling water into the teapot, and she couldn't help admiring the way he managed to make a simple domesticated task look manly.

'If you like,' he said as he set the teapot on a cane table-mat, 'I'll give Alan Davidson, the solicitor, a quick call and ask if there's any need for you to show up. It'll only take a tick.'

Kate offered a mystified smile. 'If you insist, but I hope I'm not needed. I'm dreadfully tired.'

'The tea will refresh you. Do you mind helping yourself?'

'Not at all,' she told his departing back.

She poured a mug of tea. It was a strong brew and

piping hot. She added milk and sugar, took her mug to the window and sipped hot tea while she looked out at the scattering of farm sheds and the dry, thirsty paddocks.

This property—named Radnor by Kate's grandfather after his beloved Radnor Hills in England—didn't look like a prize inheritance now, in the middle of a drought.

But she could remember her uncle's boast that, when the rains returned, the Channel Country provided some of the best grazing land in Queensland. One good wet season could change the entire district in a matter of weeks.

Mighty river systems with strangely exotic names like Barcoo, Bulloo and Diamantina would bring water from the north, spreading into tributaries, into hundreds of creeks and billabongs, like blood filling arteries, drenching the hungry earth and bringing it back to life.

People who lived here needed faith to ride out the tough times until the good rains returned and thick feed covered the ground once more. Kate's mother, sequestered in England, had never understood that.

Noah, on the other hand, knew it implicitly.

Kate drank more tea and sighed heavily. She was deathly tired. Jet lag was making her head spin. And she still felt a crushing disappointment at missing the funeral.

Footsteps sounded in the passage and she turned to see Noah coming through the doorway, his grey eyes unreadable, his mouth a straight, inscrutable line. 'Alan Davidson was most definite. You should attend the reading of the will.'

Kate shook her head in annoyance. Didn't people around here understand about jet lag? She couldn't bear the thought of bouncing back down that bumpy road into Jindabilla. 'I'm too tired,' she said, and she yawned widely to prove it. 'I'll probably fall asleep in the middle of the reading.'

'Take another mug of tea to your room and rest for an hour.' Noah spoke quietly, but with an unmistakable air of authority. 'Feel free to use the bathroom across the passage from your room. But be ready to leave at two-thirty.'

Kate knew she'd been given an order.

CHAPTER TWO

NOAH shifted uncomfortably on the hard wooden chair in the solicitor's office, and watched a lonely ceiling fan struggle to bring relief to the over-dressed group in the crowded room. Neck ties were a rarity in the summer heat, but he and Alan Davidson had worn them today out of respect for their good friend, Angus.

James Calloway, Liane's city lawyer, had gone one better and was wearing a spiffy business suit and a striped bow-tie that looked suspiciously like those worn by the old boys' clubs of Sydney's private schools. James was, Noah noted, very red in the face.

Old Angus would be chuckling if he could see this mob, suffering on his behalf.

But Noah had little to laugh about. He'd been through one hell of a week—the shock of Angus's sudden death, the heart-rending task of spreading the sad news, the struggle to focus on arrangements for the funeral and a fitting farewell. And then, everything had been soured by his ex-wife's unexpected appearance in Jindabilla with her fancy lawyer in tow.

The nerve of Liane—showing up out of the blue and coming to the funeral, as if she didn't know that old

Angus had, in the end, despised her and blamed her for bringing unhappiness to the people he loved.

She was still causing trouble. Noah couldn't forgive her for neglecting to pass on Kate Brodie's message. It was beyond embarrassing that Angus's niece had travelled all the way from England and had missed everything. The minister could easily have held the funeral off for another day or two.

But it was just as sickening to discover that Liane was here now for the reading of the will. What the hell did she think she was up to? She'd cleaned him out during the divorce. What more could she want? The question made Noah's jaw clench so tightly his teeth threatened to crack.

Alan Davidson shuffled the papers on his desk and looked tentatively around at the gathering. He gave a quiet nod to Noah, and a poor attempt at a friendly smile to Kate, who was sitting stiffly to one side near the window, as if she wanted to separate herself from the rest of them. And who, thought Noah, could blame her?

He let his gaze rest on her—an extremely pleasant distraction. She was dressed simply in a cream blouse and a brown linen skirt. Sunlight, streaming through the wooden slats of the blinds, shot fiery lights into her whisky-coloured hair and added a pink glow to her delicate English complexion. Her eyes were the softest shade of green.

Back at the homestead, she'd looked washed out, a pale shadow of the lively, flirtatious girl who'd come here for a holiday. But, given her long journey and jet lag, that wasn't surprising.

Now, sitting in the golden beams of afternoon light, with her autumn hair and her brown skirt, she looked tranquil and undeniably eye-catching. Like a sexy version of a Rembrandt painting.

Alan Davidson opened the folder in front of him, snapping Noah roughly back to the business at hand. Noah's fingers reached for the knot of his tie, and he longed to loosen it to relieve the sudden strangling sensation that clawed at his throat.

He had no reason to be nervous, and yet he couldn't shake the feeling that something was wrong.

Watching Noah's restlessness, Kate wished she was anywhere but here. It wasn't just jet lag making her so ill at ease. She could have cut the tension in the room with a knife. In spite of his suntan, Noah looked pale, and he kept shifting in his chair. Now he was sitting ramrod straight, with his jaw clenched and his hands fisted on his knees, his knuckles white.

Her heart went out to him. She knew he'd loved her uncle as deeply as any son could, and he was still grappling with his grief. But at least he would walk out of this office today as the new owner of Radnor cattle station. Uncle Angus had told her mother years ago not to expect anything from him because it would all go to Noah. So why did Noah look so worried now?

Did he sense, as she did, that something wasn't right? Alan Davidson, the balding, middle-aged solicitor, shouldn't have been worried, but he looked almost as uneasy as Noah. He kept adjusting his glasses and opening his document folder, then closing it again.

The cocky man in the city suit—who'd been introduced as James Calloway, Liane's lawyer from Sydney—was on edge in a different way. He had an air of contained expectation, and he kept sending Liane sneaky sideways winks, almost as if he knew something the others didn't. Kate disliked his smugness and the way he kept inspecting his super-clean fingernails.

The only person in the room who looked relaxed was Noah's former wife. Liane had speedily found the most comfortable chair in the room, and she sat now with an easy elegance that displayed her long legs and expensive dress to their best advantage.

She was exceptionally pretty—very fair and very slim with bright-blue eyes fringed by long, dark lashes. Model-perfect looks, Kate decided, with that particular air of feminine awareness that brought men to their knees. Poor Noah. He must have loved her desperately. Maybe he still did?

As Kate watched, Liane leaned towards her lawyer and rested her perfectly manicured hand on his knee. Was James Calloway her lover now, or did Liane like to tease?

At last, the solicitor made a throat-clearing sound to break the silence.

'Ladies and gentlemen,' he said quietly, 'Thank you for coming here today.' He placed his square hands on the folder in front of him. 'I have in my possession two wills for Angus Harrington. One that was made many years ago, and another that was drawn up three months ago.'

He looked at them over the top of his glasses. No one spoke or moved, but Kate felt a new ripple of disquiet spread through the room, as if a stone had been dropped into a pond, disrupting its smooth surface.

'I'll cut to the chase and provide a summary.' Alan Davidson lifted a sheet from the papers in front of him. 'The property of Radnor, its buildings, stock, vehicles and equipment, were Angus Harrington's only assets.'

As he spoke, the solicitor let his gaze shift from person to person in the room. 'There were some cash reserves, but those funds have been depleted by the long drought. There won't be much left in the bank by the time the final debts and mortgages are settled.'

He paused, looked down at the papers, then directed his attention to Noah. 'Noah, Angus left you a half-share of Radnor, its assets and its debts.'

A half-share?

Kate saw the flare of shock in Noah's eyes.

She was shocked too. And confused. What did this mean?

The solicitor turned quickly to Kate. 'Ms Brodie.'

Her hand flew to her throat and her heart began to thump mercilessly.

'It was your uncle's wish that you should inherit the other half of his estate.'

'No,' she whispered.

Alan Davidson frowned.

'No.' Kate shook her head. 'There must be a mistake.'

'Of course it's a mistake!' cried Liane. 'That can't possibly be right.'

Grim faced, the solicitor held out the sheet of paper, pointing with his finger to the appropriate words, but they swam before Kate's eyes. She felt vague and confused, as if this was happening to someone else.

'Ms Brodie,' Alan said. 'In the revised will, your uncle's intention was quite clear. In fact, his insistence that you be included as a beneficiary is the reason the will was changed.'

Stunned, Kate looked from the solicitor to Noah's stony face. This didn't make sense. She couldn't possibly own half of an Australian cattle property. Why on earth would her uncle do that?

Why would he do it to Noah?

Before she could find the words to frame a question, Noah's ex-wife leapt to her feet.

'James, you told me you could get *me* half of everything Noah inherited. How can this little biddy from England sneak though the back door and take my share?'

Hands on hips, Liane darted fiery sneers at them all. 'I'm entitled to a half-share of that property. I wasted the best years of my life in that ghastly place, living under the same roof as that awful old man.'

Calloway reached for her hand and tried to pull her back down into her chair, but she shook him away.

'Noah owes me, and he knows it. They can't do this to me. It's ridiculous. I want my money.'

Noah, darkly furious, refused to respond.

Kate watched from her seat, mortified. She felt responsible for this fiasco. But utterly helpless. She hadn't *asked* for an inheritance. What *had* Uncle Angus been thinking?

As she sat, wondering what on earth she should say or do, the door from the outer office began to open. Just a crack at first, and then wider, and one half of a small face appeared.

The door inched open wider and Kate saw a little girl aged about seven or eight. She was fair-skinned and petite, with freckles across her nose and wavy, light brown hair that almost reached her shoulders. Her eyes were the exact shade of grey as Noah's eyes, but right now they were round with worry and fixed on Liane.

Kate wondered if she was Olivia, Noah and Liane's daughter. Perhaps she'd been told to wait outside. Had she been upset by the high-pitched agitation in her mother's voice?

Liane hadn't noticed the child and she continued to

rant. 'On your feet, James! You'll have to start calling your people in Sydney. I want this matter settled right now.'

With that, Calloway was hauled unceremoniously out of his chair.

Kate rose, too, but in a more dignified manner. She swallowed nervously. 'I don't understand my uncle's decision. I'm as shocked as anyone else. But it might be easier for you to discuss this complication if I wait outside.'

Liane glared at her suspiciously.

Noah looked as if he might have spoken, but Kate gestured to the small figure in the doorway. 'The little girl.'

Noah's head whipped round and, when he saw her, his face morphed into a mix of delight and despair.

Liane snapped at the child. 'I told you to wait outside!'

The girl's eyes grew huge. Her mouth trembled, and she looked very much as if she was about to burst into tears.

'I could wait with her,' Kate volunteered.

Noah sent her a look of immense gratitude, while Liane gave a little annoyed huff and shrugged her shoulders impatiently. 'Whatever.'

Relieved to escape, Kate shut the office door behind her and drew a deep breath. She wished, rather recklessly given the circumstances, that the ownership of Radnor could be settled by the time this door opened again.

She smiled at the little girl. 'Hello,' she said warmly as she held out her hand. 'We haven't met, but I've heard about you, Olivia. I'm Kate. I'm a friend of your—of your father's.'

'Hello.' Olivia did not offer her hand and she didn't return Kate's smile. She looked again at the closed door separating her from her parents.

The voices on the other side were mostly muffled, except for Liane's high-pitched, angry demands.

'Why are they fighting?' Olivia asked. 'What's happening in there?'

'It's a business discussion. And I'm afraid business can get rather complicated at times.'

Kate nodded towards a long, pew-like seat against the opposite wall. 'Shall we wait there?'

Olivia shook her head. 'I'm tired of sitting. I've been sitting for ages 'n' ages.'

A quick flick through the reading material on the coffee table showed Kate that none of it was suitable for children. She wondered if she should try to tell the little girl a story, but story telling wasn't really her forte.

Olivia pointed to the open door leading out to the sunlit street. 'Can we go outside?'

'Well…' Aware of the heated discussion on the other side of the door, Kate made a snap decision. 'Why not? I don't suppose anyone will mind.' After all, Jindabilla was a very tiny country town, hardly more than one wide, dusty main street. No chance of getting lost.

The little girl was already skipping towards the door. 'There's a beautiful pig out there.' Her eyes were shining suddenly.

'A pig?' *Good grief.* What a quantum leap, to come from discussing wills and inheritances to pigs.

On the footpath, Kate shaded her gaze against the sun's glare. 'Where is this pig?'

'In the back of that blue ute outside the pub.'

Even if Olivia hadn't described the utility truck so accurately, Kate could hardly miss the stream of snuffling oinks and squeals.

Her head was whirling. She was still stunned by her uncle's will, still feeling Noah's shock. She glanced back to the solicitor's office. What was going on in there? What had they decided?

'Can't you hear him?' Olivia cried, giving Kate's hand a tug.

'Of course I can.' Kate smiled. '*And* I can see him.' A distinctly piggy snout and a dirty pink trotter appeared over the ute's tray back.

'He's so cute! Lift me up! I want to see him properly.'

The little girl's reticence was a thing of the past, and she held her arms up to Kate as if they'd been best friends for ever.

Kate couldn't help suspecting that Liane would object to her daughter being lifted up to admire a pig, but she was charmed by the child's eagerness—so different from the worry in her eyes a few moments earlier. She hoisted Olivia onto her hip and together they peered at the small pink pig that looked up at them with pale, expectant eyes.

'Isn't he gorgeous?'

'He is rather cute,' Kate admitted.

Olivia's face was a picture of enraptured adoration. With one skinny arm around Kate's neck, she reached out with the other to pat the top of the little pig's head. 'Daddy says that pigs are terribly clever. They're much cleverer than cows, and they're even cleverer than dogs.'

'I didn't know that. But I've heard they make great pets.'

Olivia beamed at her joyously. 'This one's so handsome; I want to call him Baby Prince Charming.'

Kate laughed. 'Why not? I couldn't imagine a better name for him.'

The pig squealed and snuffled, and Olivia made oinking noises back at him. But eventually she grew heavy, and Kate set her back on the footpath.

She half-expected the child to protest, but Olivia took her hand in a gesture of such innocent trust that Kate felt a lump in her throat. 'Are—are pigs your favourite animal?' she asked.

'Probably.' A wistful expression came over her little face. 'When I lived with Daddy, we had lots and lots of animals—piglets and chickens and ducklings and calves.'

'And puppies?'

'Lots of puppies.' Her bottom lip drooped. 'I can't have pets any more.'

'Because you live in the city?'

She nodded. 'Mummy said we're not allowed to have any pets in our apartment. Not even a goldfish.'

Kate understood Olivia's disappointment. Her own mother had never been fond of animals, and she felt a rush of sympathy for the child. After the rustic casualness of life in an Outback homestead, where sticky fingers posed no threat and a puppy on the couch were the norm, it would be very hard to get used to a slick and shiny city apartment.

'But you must have all kinds of exciting things to do in the city,' she suggested diplomatically.

'Not really. Sydney's boring.'

Before Kate could respond, Liane's voice sounded shrilly behind them. She turned to see the child's mother and James Calloway charging down the footpath.

Completely ignoring Kate, Liane thrust her hand towards her daughter. 'Come along now,' she ordered with an imperious tilt of her chin.

A fleeting expression that might have been fear flickered over the little girl's face, but it was gone so quickly Kate decided that she must have imagined it.

'We've found a pig,' Olivia told her mother.

'Good God.' Liane's lips curled in an expression of distaste. She gave another impatient shake of her outstretched hand. 'Now, come on, Olivia. We've got to get back to the motel. We have a lot of important phone calls to make.'

The little girl hesitated and chewed her lip. 'Can I stay tonight with Daddy?'

'No, of course you can't.' Her mother rolled her eyes. 'First thing in the morning we're getting out of this dump and back home to Sydney.' She grabbed the little girl's hand. 'Come on, now. No nonsense.'

Rising quickly onto tiptoes, Olivia whispered to Kate, 'Can you say goodbye to Baby Prince Charming for me?'

'Of course,' Kate whispered back. 'I promise.'

Her smile faltered as she watched the trio—mother, daughter and sharp Sydney lawyer—hurry away down the dusty footpath. As they rounded a corner, Olivia looked back, just once, over her shoulder, and lifted her hand to send Kate a quick wave. 'Say goodbye to Daddy too,' she called.

Kate was surprised by how flat she felt as she went back inside. The door to Alan Davidson's office was open, and she could see both men in there, still busy talking and looking extremely solemn.

When she knocked, Noah turned, and her heart seemed to slip a little; he looked incredibly handsome in spite of the bleakness of his expression.

'Am I intruding?' she asked.

'No, of course not. You have a stake in this. Come on in.' Noah stood, and with a gentlemanly gesture she couldn't ever remember her boyfriend using he drew out a chair for her.

'Thank you.'

'How's Olivia?' Noah's eyes gleamed with a bright warmth that sent a tremor through Kate as she sat.

'She's fine. She was very excited because there's a pig in the street outside. In the back of a ute.'

'A pig?' Noah's smile lit up his face.

'A baby pig. Very cute.'

He laughed briefly. 'She'd love that.'

Kate watched the way his eyes sparkled, then almost immediately turned misty. Clearly, joy and pain were part and parcel of his relationship with his daughter. She wondered how often he saw Olivia, how much time they had together. Somehow, she couldn't imagine Liane going out of her way to make access easy.

Rubbing a hand over his face, as if to clear his thoughts, Noah sobered and returned to business. 'I was just telling Alan I had no idea this inheritance could be so complicated,' he said. 'I'm afraid I'm still trying to get my head around it.'

'So nothing's settled?'

Alan Davidson took his spectacles off and offered Kate a teeth-gritted version of a smile. 'I've explained to Noah that, with a firm like Calloway and Brandon behind her, Liane has a very good chance of pushing her claim for a half-share through the courts.'

'But I thought—?' Kate wasn't quite sure how to put her question. 'I assumed everything about the divorce had been finalised.'

Alan nodded. 'That's right. But Liane has twelve months after the decree absolute to file for property set-tlement. She can mount a case about her involvement at Radnor during her marriage, citing her contribution during the five-and-a-half years that she lived there, and her input into the running of the place.'

Kate could see why the courts would allow this. She knew nothing about the reasons for Noah and Liane's divorce, but it made sense that a woman might need protection in certain circumstances.

She frowned. 'But if Liane claims her half of Noah's share, or half of his *half*-share, does that mean that Noah will end up with only a quarter of the estate?'

The solicitor nodded grimly. 'A quarter of a drought-stricken estate at that.'

What a shock for Noah! Kate knew he'd expected to inherit Radnor intact, and now even his half-share would be whittled away. After he'd worked so hard on Radnor all his life, it seemed terribly unfair.

'I don't understand,' she said, unable to keep a lid on her thoughts. 'Why on earth has Uncle Angus given half of Radnor to me? It just doesn't make any kind of sense.'

The men seemed unwilling or unable to answer her and, in the silence, the ceiling fan creaked as it circled slowly.

At last, Alan said, 'Perhaps your uncle was being canny. It's no secret that he never got on with Liane, and he may have anticipated that she could put in her claim for a half-share. He might have done this to frustrate her.'

Kate gave a helpless shake of her head. 'You mean Angus didn't want Liane to inherit half his property? But couldn't Noah have bought her out?'

The two men exchanged a silent glance.

Noah said, 'Given the drought, the banks aren't very generous with their loans. I might have been forced to sell up the lot to meet Liane's claims.'

'Oh.'

He shrugged. 'Now, with this new will, whatever

happens half of Radnor stays in the family.' His cool, faintly amused glance flickered over Kate.

To her dismay, her cheeks grew hot. Irrationally, she found herself remembering how very, *very* different Noah's smile had been all those years ago, when she was seventeen... Just before he kissed her.

But it was feeble to remember that now.

Angry at her weakness, she spoke too loudly. 'I'm sorry, but I know nothing about cattle, or running Outback properties in Australia. I'm quite prepared to say that I'm not entitled to a half-share in Radnor. It's your home, Noah. Not mine.'

'That's not how it works,' he said quietly.

She cast a frantic glance over the pile of papers on Alan Davidson's desk, at his bookcases filled with expensively bound legal tomes. Surely lawyers knew clever ways to get round this kind of problem?

She was grateful that her boyfriend was safely tucked away on the other side of the world. As a man of finance, he would be horrified if he knew what she planned to say next. 'I can hand my half back, can't I? Give my share to Noah? I'm sure you know a way to devise some sensible arrangement.'

'That is *not* going to happen.' Noah spoke with such vehemence that Kate flinched. He scowled at her. 'You don't know what you're saying, Kate.'

'I know exactly what I'm saying.'

His face was dark, his mouth tight and hard, frighteningly hard. 'No one hands over half an inheritance like Radnor.'

'I can if I wish.'

Cursing beneath his breath, Noah leaned forward, eyes blazing. 'Don't be a fool. Radnor might have been blighted by drought for the better part of five years, but the property's still valuable. All it takes is one good wet season. It's over half a million acres.'

She gasped. That much? The scope of it was beyond imagining.

'Even if that means nothing to you, Kate, I intend to respect Angus's wishes. He obviously wanted you to have a half-share.'

'That's what I don't understand,' she said softly. 'I know I'm his niece, but he looked on you as—as his son.'

'Angus's mind was perfectly sound.' Noah spoke now with quiet resignation. 'He knew exactly what he was doing, and he must have thought very carefully before changing his will.'

Perhaps it was her tiredness that made Kate angry. She wanted to stamp her feet, to yell at Noah, to urge him to stop being stubborn. How could he give up so easily? He'd worked so hard for Radnor.

Alan coughed discreetly. 'If you hand your share over to Noah, Kate, there will be even more for Liane to claim.'

'That's true,' said Kate quietly. In other words, she could be of more help to Noah if she retained her share. 'But if Noah wants to stay on Radnor he must buy Liane out, mustn't he? That's what she'll want, isn't it— money rather than land?'

Alan pursed his lips. 'Noah may not have a big enough share of the Radnor asset to raise the necessary money.'

'Are you saying he'll *still* be forced to sell up his share just to settle her claim?'

Kate was horrified. This was ridiculous. Noah had been born at Radnor. It was his home. His life. The very thought of him wandering about the Outback, looking for another job, starting again from scratch, was ludicrous!

Impulsively, she said, 'We have no choice, then. Noah and I will have to form a partnership.'

Noah stared at Kate as if she'd grown a third ear.

To her eternal shame, she blushed again. 'I—I m-mean a b-business partnership, of course. Then the partnership could buy Liane's share. The banks wouldn't turn down a proposal like that, would they?'

'That's generous,' Noah said quietly. 'But I won't accept it.'

'Hey!' Alan suddenly turned on Noah. 'Wake up, man. It's only a business arrangement. Not marriage.'

Marriage?

Zap! To Kate's horror her already hot cheeks turned fiery.

Noah's chair scraped on the wooden floor, and he jumped to his feet. 'What kind of fool comment is that?'

'I was joking, of course,' Alan quickly back-pedalled. He sent Kate a quick wink. 'That's how it would have happened in the good old days, of course. A quick, arranged marriage and, hey presto, everyone's problems are solved.'

Kate was dismayed that Noah's reaction was getting to her. Why did he have to make it so obvious that he was horrified by Alan's light-hearted suggestion? She'd got the message nine years ago that he had no romantic interest in her.

To cover the awkwardness, Alan made a business of tidying the papers on his desk, setting them straight inside the folder. 'You should both take a few days to think about this.'

Noah had moved to the door, one shoulder leaning on the jamb, his hands thrust deep in his pockets. He looked tired, as tired as Kate felt.

'You're right,' he said quietly. 'We need a few days. You're jet lagged, Kate. You're in no condition to be making rash offers. You need to get back to the house and have a good, long sleep. You'll probably come to your senses in the morning.'

CHAPTER THREE

FROM habit Noah woke just before dawn.

He'd slept soundly, which was a surprise, as he'd been troubled by bad dreams ever since he'd found Angus slumped at his desk, ashen-faced and unconscious.

Now, grey dawn light seeped into his bedroom. Familiar details of the room came to life: the timber-framed window, the roll-top desk in the corner, the faded photo of his parents, the old pine chest of drawers...

Then he remembered.

He was going to lose all of this. He was going to lose his home. Lose Radnor.

He sat up quickly, fighting hot panic—caused not by a nightmare this time but by sickening reality.

With a groan, he threw his bedclothes aside, strode naked to the window and looked out at the flat, treeless landscape spreading endlessly, as far as the eye could see.

A terrible sense of loss flooded him. He was twenty-nine years old and he'd been born here. Not counting the years he'd spent at boarding school, this was the only home he'd ever known. He'd travelled, of course. He'd covered most of Australia and he'd seen prettier places— grander landscapes...richer country...

But a soul-deep love of these sparse, flat plains flowed in his veins. This country might be subject to drought, but its strength lay in its ability to rejuvenate. The rain would come eventually, and tenacity to weather the drought was part of the strength of the people who lived here.

Noah had that strength, that patience. And Angus had known it, damn it. But the old fox had tied up his will so that half of this property went to an English girl who'd been here once, almost a decade ago, for a brief holiday.

Noah jerked his gaze from the view and went through to his small adjoining bathroom.

Any normal guy would harbour resentment, he told himself as he palmed lather onto his jaw. He should be thinking about Kate Brodie with animosity and bitterness.

Not with hot-blooded lust.

He shouldn't be remembering the last time she'd been here, the way he'd kissed her, and the way she'd responded. Hell, if he hadn't had Angus's warning ringing in his head, who knew what might have happened back then?

Angus had started bellowing orders even before Kate had arrived. At the time, it had nearly killed Noah to ignore Kate. He'd been completely smitten by her flashing green eyes, perfect skin and all that shiny red-gold hair. And her smile.

He'd broken down once and given into his need to taste Kate's smiling lips, to touch her soft, warm, milk-white skin.

One kiss, despite Angus Harrington's warning…

'Hands off her, do you hear me? If you lay so much as a finger on my sister's daughter, I'll never forgive you, son.'

Son. For as long as Noah could remember, Angus had called him that. He'd been four at the time of his parents' accident, and could barely remember them. His only memory was based on the photo on his dresser. His father, long-legged and dark, and no doubt smelling of dust and cigarettes, was leaning against the stock rails and grinning at his mother. She had a soft, heart-shaped face and pretty, pale-brown hair. Like Olivia's.

Olivia. Noah grimaced and picked up the razor. He couldn't afford to think about Olivia now, on top of everything else. Losing her, losing Radnor. Hell, any minute he'd start bawling.

He began to scrape with the razor, making dark tracks over his jaw through the white foam. But his thoughts winged straight back to Kate Brodie.

She'd changed a great deal. Matured was the word to use, he supposed. She had grown quieter. More serious. Even more attractive and womanly.

Last night on the way home from Jindabilla she'd slept, which should have been fine. Noah had been grateful that she hadn't wanted to carry on about Angus's will. But she'd been so sleepy she'd ended up with her head on his shoulder, which meant he'd driven all those miles with the fragrance of her freshly shampooed hair filling his nostrils, with the warm pressure of her soft cheek against his shoulder, and the gentle hush of her breath on his neck.

And, when they'd reached the homestead, Kate had been so out of it that he'd had to help her inside. She'd leaned sleepily against him as they'd negotiated the stairs, with his arm about her slender waist, and he'd been super-conscious of her curves above and below.

Once Kate had changed and was ready for bed, he'd taken her hot cocoa, just as he might have done for Olivia.

Big mistake. Huge. How could he have been such an idiot? He'd found Kate in bed in a silky nightdress of skimpy cream silk with lace trims and thin straps, hair sleep-tumbled, eyelashes drooping. She'd blushed profusely and muttered apologies as she accepted the cocoa.

Remembering how she'd looked made him…

Damn. He nicked his jaw.

It was too long since he'd been with a woman.

But Kate Brodie was not the solution to that particular problem, Noah decided as he jutted his jaw and dabbed at the nick with the corner of a towel.

Why on earth had Alan Davidson let fly yesterday with that crazy comment about a marriage of convenience? He must have known that Noah couldn't contemplate any kind of marriage after the messy divorce he'd just been through. Hell. Maybe Alan had been running every option through his bloody legal brain—but did he have to voice the crazy ones?

As for Kate's suggestion that they form a business partnership, she'd been talking off the top of her head without really thinking it through. Very soon she'd come to her senses and realise that the last thing she wanted was to have her life tied up in a cattle station on the other side of the world.

The sooner she went back to England, the better.

He'd work out a way to solve his own problems, without getting tangled up with Angus's niece. She'd been trouble enough last time she'd come to Radnor.

Kate tossed and turned. She'd been awake for what felt like ages, her body clock disoriented and her mind churning over the events of yesterday. The questions buzzed in her head like maddened flies. Why had Angus Harrington made such an unexpected bequest? What did he want from her? What was he hoping?

It was such an astonishing legacy. Bewildering.

She found herself wondering if Alan Davidson had been right when he'd suggested that Angus had left her half of Radnor to protect his property from Noah's divorced wife. And, if that was so, what had he hoped Kate would do about it now?

Could he possibly expect her to live here, to run Radnor with Noah?

Poor Angus. He wouldn't have made such a mistake if he'd known their history. If only she'd had the courage to confide in her uncle. Over the years, she'd sent him letters, but she'd only ever told Angus about her fascination for Australia, for his cattle property and his life-style. Not a word about Noah.

If Angus Harrington had known how silly she'd been, he might not have pushed them into this awkward partnership.

Wincing as her mind came back to this dead end for the hundredth time, Kate leapt out of bed. She checked her mobile, but there were no messages.

It would be early evening in England. She tried phoning her mother, but she was out, so she left a message that she'd arrived safely and all was well. Kate didn't mention her surprise inheritance. She needed to speak to her mother in person about that. She dialled again and got through to Derek's mobile.

She kept her voice low so that she didn't wake Noah. 'Hi there, Derek, it's Kate.'

'Oh, really? Where are you?'

'In Australia.' What a strange question. Where else

would she be? She wished Derek didn't sound so put out. 'I just wanted to let you know I made it here safely.'

'Sorry. Can you speak up?'

She could hear laughter and music in the background.

'How long do you think you'll be in Australia?' Derek asked, raising his voice to reach her over the noise.

Wishing she'd gone outside to make this call, Kate spoke as loudly as she dared. 'I'm still not sure. Not very long, I guess, but there have been complications.'

It would be good to tell Derek about her inheritance. His experience in the banking world could be helpful, and he'd be sure to offer great advice about business partnerships. But if Derek was at a party...

'Can I hear people speaking in German?' she asked.

'What? Oh, can you hear that? Yes, there's a table of Germans close by.'

'Are you down at the pub?'

This was met by a marked hesitation on the other end of the line, more than the normal time lapse on an international call. 'No.' Derek sounded uneasy. 'I'm in—eh—Birmingham. It's a business thing—I'm with clients.'

It was a clear dismissal. Derek was busy and didn't want to chat, and Kate tried hard not to mind. 'I'd better not keep you, then.'

They said goodbye and she disconnected, and knew she was silly to feel dissatisfied. If Derek was busy with clients she could hardly expect a romantic chat. Anyway, sweet talk had never been his style.

Just the same...

She sighed. Perhaps Derek was stressed. He often got stressed about his job, and it was probably tension rather than impatience that she'd heard in his voice. A yawn escaped her, and she realised she hadn't had nearly enough sleep. But there was no point in going back to bed. Noah would be up and about soon. What she needed was a shower to freshen her up.

She was sorting through her things, trying to choose suitable clothes for a hot, sticky day in the Outback, when footsteps sounded on the veranda outside her room and then there was a knock at the French doors. Kate opened them a chink.

'Morning, Kate.'

Noah's dark hair was damp, his rugged jaw clean and smooth as if he'd just shaved, and there was a nick just below his ear. Kate could smell the tang of his after-shave, and she had to clutch the door frame for support when he gave her a slow smile.

'Is it too early for you for breakfast?' he asked.

'Not at all.' She was annoyed by how suddenly breath-less she sounded. 'I can be ready in a jiffy. I'll come and help you.'

He shrugged. 'No need to rush. But you didn't eat last night, so I'm thinking you'll need the works—a full cooked breakfast.'

She was smiling through her quick shower, and while she changed into linen shorts and a T-shirt and then hurried down the hallway.

Divine smells were coming from the kitchen. More disturbingly divine was the sight of Noah at the stove. *Oh, help.* A woman was not supposed to finish a phone call with her boyfriend and immediately go weak at the knees at the sight of another man.

How was it possible that Noah could look so super-attractive standing at a kitchen stove, turning sausages? Maybe she was still affected by jet lag. Or the heat. Or maybe it was something to do with the clothes these

Outback guys wore—Noah's low-slung jeans and rumpled cotton shirt.

Heavens. What was wrong with her? How could she be so fickle? Hastily, she tried to substitute Derek into this scene—Derek wearing those battered jeans and nonchalantly flipping sausages and eggs at half-past six in the morning.

Somehow, the picture wouldn't gel. Derek was a night owl and he hated mornings. In fact, he hated cooking, and he rarely wore jeans. He was more the pinstriped-suit type.

This is not going to be a repeat of the last time I was here.

Kate's insides flinched as she remembered the pain of getting over her infatuation with Noah. Her skin flushed from head to toe as she remembered her embarrassing behaviour. And then to think she'd still sent him a Valentine's card shortly after her return.

Oh, cringe. How could she have been so stupid? Noah had never replied, of course, and she hoped to high heaven he'd forgotten it. Keen to switch her thoughts to *anything* but that, she asked brightly, 'Shall I make toast?'

'Sure.' Noah gestured with an elbow. 'Toaster's over in the corner. Bread's in the box. Butter in the fridge.'

His casualness brought her back to earth. Not only was she shallow and fickle, she was totally pathetic. She had no place in her life for romantic fantasies about Noah Carmody.

First, she had Derek. Second, she really had learned her lesson last time. Crumbs. Maybe she needed to write it out a hundred times: *I am not Noah's type. I am not Noah's type.*

While the bread was toasting, Kate found place mats

and cutlery, set two places at one end of the big pine table, and added mugs for the pot of piping-hot tea.

She didn't think she could possibly eat the huge plateful Noah set in front of her, but she was actually ravenous, and the sausages were crisp on the outside and juicy and savoury in the middle. As for the bacon…

Noah grinned when he saw her empty plate. 'I like to see a girl with an appetite.'

'That was delicious,' she said. 'Thank you.'

She was about to offer to wash up when he frowned and stood, head turned, as if he was listening to something outside. 'There's a car coming.'

At first Kate couldn't hear a thing, but then she caught the faint drone of a motor in the distance.

Noah, carrying his mug of tea, went to the row of windows and looked out, eyes narrowed. 'It isn't a truck. It's a smaller car.'

'Shall I make a fresh pot of tea?'

Kate was about to reach for the kettle when he held up his hand. 'Hold on. I don't think this is a social visit.'

Although Noah stood quietly, shoulders relaxed, taking another sip from his mug, Kate sensed a new tension in him as he watched the visitor's approach. She moved to the bank of windows, curious now, but she couldn't possibly identify the vehicle making the cloud of white dust as it came towards them.

Beside her, Noah exclaimed softly, 'It's the police.'

With an economy of movement, he set the mug on the table and went out onto the veranda. Kate couldn't help noticing that he made an art form of the loose-hipped, long-legged stride of the Outback cattleman.

Stop it. She gathered up their breakfast things and took them to the sink, and watched through the window while she rinsed the dishes. A white station wagon with distinctive blue-and-white-chequered markings emerged out of the cloud of dust. Squinting against the bright morning sun, Kate could just make out a small figure on the front seat beside the driver.

As soon as the car had crossed the home paddock and pulled up at the bottom of the steps, the passenger door opened and Olivia leapt out and flew up the steps, her pale brown hair streaming behind her like ribbons.

'Daddy!' the child sobbed as she flung herself at Noah.

What on earth could have happened?

Kate hurried to the veranda as her mind skidded through alarming possibilities. Noah looked as shocked as she felt. Crouching swiftly, he gripped his daughter by the shoulders, his gaze fierce as he searched her tear-stained face for clues.

'What's the matter? What's happened?'

The child simply shook her head and burst into tears. Surely there hadn't been an accident?

The policeman, a stout fellow in his fifties, got out of the driver's seat stiffly, donned his cap and sauntered around the front of his car.

'Morning, Noah,' he drawled.

'Stan, for goodness' sake, what's happened?'

'Your little girl's mother reported her missing from their motel suite. I found her out on the highway, but when I tried to take her back into town she put on such a turn I thought I'd better bring her out here to you.'

'She was on the highway?'

'Found her just past the turn off, west of Jindabilla.'

'Liv, for heaven's sake.' Noah's voice was choked.

The policeman removed his hat and fiddled with the brim. 'I've notified her mother, and she's already on her way out here. I guess you and your ex will have to sort this out between you, Noah.'

'Yes, of course.' The muscles in Noah's throat jerked as he stood and shook hands with the policeman. 'Thank you, Stan.' His voice was subdued, shaken. 'I hate to think what might have happened if you hadn't found Liv.'

He turned back to his daughter. 'Why did you run away, Liv?'

Olivia's head hung low.

'Tell me,' Noah insisted.

'Are you angry?' she asked in a very small voice.

He dragged a deep breath; let it out on a sigh. 'No. I'm not angry. Just worried.'

'I don't want to go back to Sydney.'

Kate saw the pain in Noah's face, saw his body stiffen and his jaw clench, as if he were biting off his response. In the silence, the girl looked up at her father with fearful eyes, her little mouth trembling.

Noah's silence seemed to stretch for ever, but then a soft cry broke from him and he clasped Olivia to him.

She sobbed against his shoulder, wrapped her thin arms around his neck and clung. 'Don't make me go, Daddy. Please let me s-stay here with you.'

Noah closed his eyes, and Kate was shocked by the agony she read in his rugged face. His big hand trembled as he cradled the back of his daughter's head and held her against him.

Watching them, Kate felt her eyes sting and her throat hurt, as if she'd swallowed concrete. She could hardly remember her own father, but the memories she had were precious. She'd loved the way he used to swing her high in the air, and the way he'd called her his princess.

Oh, how she'd adored him.

Now, as she watched Noah and his daughter, she could feel the depth of their special bond and the rawness of their strained emotions. Their pain was real. This was not simply a matter of a spoiled little girl manipulating her parent.

In the distance another cloud of white dust appeared, accompanied by the growl of another motor. No doubt this was Liane.

'I'll put the kettle on,' mumbled Kate, deciding she would be wise to make herself scarce.

No one seemed to notice her departure to the kitchen. She filled the kettle and set it on the stove, then filled the sink with hot water, found detergent and began to wash up. Outside, the growl of the approaching car grew louder. Then there was a screech as it came to a halt, and a door slammed.

Liane marched to the foot of the front steps and stopped, hands on hips, painted lips pursed as she surveyed the scene on the veranda. Her blonde hair was perfectly styled, and she was wearing a fuchsia-pink dress, dark glasses and high-heeled white sandals. She looked as if she'd stepped straight out of fashion magazine.

'I hope you're happy now, Noah!'

Kate supposed she'd lived a rather sheltered life. Her father had died when she was five, so she'd never experienced domestic disputes. But her grandparents had been divorced before she was born. Her grandfather had left England with their son, Uncle Angus, while her grandmother had remained at home with Kate's mother.

The bitterness of the split had endured throughout her grandmother's life, and the subject of her grandfather had always been dismissed with a pursed mouth and a sniff. She had always wondered how such bitterness was born, and now she was seeing something very similar unfolding before her eyes. With poor little Olivia caught in the crossfire.

Kate was in the walk-in pantry, hunting for biscuits to serve if morning tea was required, when she heard Noah's footsteps crossing the kitchen.

She turned. Noah looked tired already. He smiled sadly and she felt her heart slip.

'Can I ask a favour, Kate?'

She nodded. 'How can I help?'

'I was hoping you could entertain Olivia again.' He released a small sigh. 'Liane and I need to talk. I have to try to sort this out.'

'Yes, of course.' As she said this, Kate wondered what on earth she could do to keep Noah's daughter distracted without toys or children's books. The drought-stricken paddocks were empty, so there were no small animals like Baby Prince Charming to amuse Olivia today—nothing out there except an elderly dog and four frangipani trees.

Frangipanis.

Perhaps they would do.

She took a wicker basket from a hook on the kitchen wall and went out onto the veranda. Liane had already disappeared somewhere inside the house, and Olivia was sitting alone on the top step, shoulders hunched, hugging her knees and staring off into the sun-drenched distance.

Kate sat beside her. 'Hello again.'

The little girl gave her a watery quarter-smile. 'Hello.'

'I've been thinking about picking up those fallen frangipani flowers. Would you like to help me?'

The child looked dubious. 'Why? Do you think they look untidy?'

'No,' Kate said with a laugh. 'Nothing like that. Did you know you can turn frangipani flowers upside down, so they look like beautiful ladies in ball gowns?' She stood and held out her hand. 'Come and see.'

Olivia got to her feet very slowly, but she made no attempt to take Kate's hand, or to follow her down the short flight of steps. Entertaining her wasn't going to be as easy as yesterday—Olivia was much more upset. Poor kid. She must be so confused and scared.

The sweet-smelling flowers lay scattered on the dark earth beneath the trees. Kate picked up a pristine white one, turned it over and set it upside down on her palm.

'See?' she said, holding it out for Olivia. 'The petals can be a princess's ball-gown, and then the stem is her neck.'

Looking doubtful, Olivia descended slowly. She came closer and peered at the upturned flower. 'I can see the ball gown, but where's her head?'

'Um—princesses have very small, neat heads.' Kate tapped her finger against the small, sticky nub where the frangipani had once been joined to the tree.

To her relief, Olivia accepted this explanation. She smiled and looked around at the array of flowers spread at her feet. 'They're pretty, aren't they?'

'I think so. If you like, we can find all the perfect ones without any brown spots.'

The little girl nodded, but when she looked up at Kate again her grey eyes narrowed. 'Are you my daddy's new girlfriend?'

'Good heavens, no!' Deeply embarrassed, Kate felt a spurt of self-righteous anger. What had she done to deserve this? 'What makes you think I'm his girlfriend?'

'You're kind and pretty.'

'Well, thanks.' *I think.* 'But that doesn't make me

your father's girlfriend. As a matter of fact,' she added as a hasty afterthought, 'I already have a boyfriend back in England.'

'So why are you here?'

'Angus was my uncle, and I came all the way from England because I wanted to go to his funeral.'

'Oh.' Olivia stood for a minute, digesting this, then she crouched to touch a velvet-soft petal with her fingertips. She picked up the flower, held it to her nose, sniffed it, and turned it over the way Kate had.

Feeling calmer now that the matter of boyfriends was settled, Kate said, 'I know flowers aren't as exciting as a baby pig.'

'They're lovely.' Olivia's smile deepened, and sweet dimples formed in her cheeks. 'Can I play with them?'

'Of course.' Kate handed over the basket, and together they gathered fragrant blooms and took a basketful back to the shady veranda.

That was where Noah found them an hour and a half later.

Kate was sitting in a deep cane chair with a magazine, which she wasn't really reading, and Olivia was on the floor beside her, surrounded by flowers which she had arranged into patterns and was now merrily rearranging.

A plate with crumbs and an apple core sat on the cane table beside his daughter, as well as an empty milk-glass. Clearly, Kate had not only found a resourceful way to entertain Olivia, but she'd also given her breakfast.

Noah knew it was pointless to make comparisons, but he couldn't help being aware of the huge difference between this peaceful, happy scene and the bitter tussle he'd just endured with Liane.

He despised self-pity, but right now he felt totally depressed—as if his life had been falling apart for years, and he was Atlas, carrying the world on his shoulders. It wasn't just that his marriage had been a disaster almost from the start. Now, with that pain more or less behind him at last, he'd faced a host of other problems.

The drought was a real headache. Radnor station still carried a thousand head of cattle, and the last of the pasture was almost gone, which meant the cattle were going to die if he didn't act very soon to save them.

And then, in one short week, he'd lost the man he'd loved as a father, and he'd learned he had a better than average chance of losing the property he'd always expected to inherit.

As if these two shocks weren't enough, he'd been handed back the daughter he was sure he'd lost.

At least this last surprise was something to smile about, something to celebrate. He had assumed he'd have to struggle for fair access to his daughter. Liane knew how much he loved Liv, and he'd half-expected her to cling to their daughter just to add to his suffering.

Instead Liane had asked him to take over raising Liv. No doubt the child had become a burden that hindered Liane's high-flying lifestyle in Sydney.

Motherhood had never sat well with his wife. From the moment she'd discovered she was pregnant, she'd never been as excited as he was, and he'd missed Liv terribly after she went to Sydney.

He'd been eaten up with worry about her the whole time she'd been away, so of course he'd jumped at the chance to have her back at Radnor with him.

The irony was that having his daughter back in his life only highlighted his dilemmas—the drought and the huge black cloud hanging over his future. Had that been Liane's ploy? Was she trying to break him?

Noah shook that thought aside. He couldn't stand in the doorway all day brooding. The Outback was no place for pessimists.

He stepped onto the veranda and Kate turned, saw him and smiled.

Her smile was so amazingly pretty—green eyes sparkling, cheeks turning pink, soft lips parted.

Zap! He came to a halt as if he'd been stung by a stockwhip.

CHAPTER FOUR

WHAT was wrong?

Kate saw the dark pain in Noah's face and knew that his conversation with Liane had upset him terribly. She supposed he was still in love with his former wife, and she tried not to mind. It was none of her business if Noah cared deeply about a woman who was grasping and selfish.

He crossed the veranda towards them, crouched next to Olivia and picked up one of her flowers. As he held it to his nose, the shocked light in his eyes and the deep vertical lines on either side of his mouth lingered.

But he remembered his manners. 'Thanks for playing nanny, Kate. You've been fabulous with Liv.'

She brushed the compliment aside. 'We've had fun. I haven't played with flowery princesses for years.'

'I don't suppose you have.' His grey eyes gleamed with the beginnings of a smile, then he turned to his daughter. 'Liv, your mother and I have had a long talk.'

The little girl looked up from her game and her face tightened. 'What did Mummy say?'

Noah paused as if he were hunting for the right words. Perhaps he couldn't find them, for he said in a rush, 'She's asked me to look after you now.'

A delighted smile brightened the little girl's face, but then it crumpled almost as quickly as it had appeared. 'Will I still see her?'

'She's—' Noah's throat worked as he swallowed. 'She's going back to Sydney.'

'Without us?'

'I'll look after you, Liv.' Noah drew his daughter into his arms, nestled her head against his shoulder and kissed her forehead. 'Pumpkin, you know Mummy and I can't live together any more.'

She pressed her face into her father's broad shoulder and made sad little snuffling noises.

Noah stroked his daughter's hair. 'I promise I'll take extra-good care of you.'

Kate's heart ached for them.

The farewell was understandably tearful, but Olivia's heartbreak was somewhat lessened by Noah's promise to take her in his ute to see the cattle. He knew his daughter was mad about anything on four legs, and he needed to check on the condition of his stock, so he invited Kate to join them for the drive.

Her green eyes widened. 'I didn't realise there were any cattle left on Radnor.' She cast a surprised look out over the sun-bleached paddocks. 'What do they eat?'

'The very last of the grass,' Noah admitted. 'Most of my neighbours have already de-stocked.' He didn't add that protecting the dry country from over-grazing was part of good station management. Too much information for a girl from England.

The three left as soon as Kate and Liv had collected sun hats, long-sleeved shirts and stout shoes. Kate brought a rather fancy-looking camera, too, and she began to snap away almost as soon as the ute took off across the trackless red ground, tyres bouncing over grey hummocks of spinifex.

The effects of the drought were everywhere, but it had encroached gradually, getting slowly worse each year, and Noah was used to the dry landscape. But now, with Kate beside him, he tried to picture the country through her eyes, and knew it must look pretty grim.

They passed a large gaping waterhole, its bottom barely covered with water, and he pointed to the wide circle of trees that ringed it. 'Those river red-gums should be standing waist deep in water.'

Kate lowered her camera. 'How do you keep your cattle alive if there's not enough water?'

He grimaced. 'There's a little water left in a few of the dams and bores, but the truth is I can't keep them going here much longer.'

'What happens then? Do you have to buy in food?'

He shook his head. 'Can't really afford to.'

They topped a rise, and below them the country dipped down into a low sandy river-bed.

'There's the cows!' Olivia squealed from the back seat, and she wound down her window and leaned out, squinting against the sun's glare.

The river valley was dotted with red cattle stretching in a long, thin line to the horizon.

'By some miracle they haven't lost too much condition.' Noah frowned as he switched the motor off. 'But they'll start to go downhill any day soon.'

Liv, in the back, rattled her door handle impatiently. 'Daddy, can I get out?'

'Sure. But keep your hat on, and don't go too far.'

Liv gazed at the cattle to her heart's content, then began to hunt on the ground for her favourite river-washed stones. Kate left the truck and stood beside Noah in the scant shade of a bimble box tree.

His throat constricted. Beneath her hat brim Kate's eyes were so very sparkly, her skin so fair against the brightness of her hair.

'There's a bit more grass here,' she said. 'But it still looks very dry.' She lifted her camera and squinted through it, and clicked madly as a small mob of curious cattle stopped grazing quietly and lumbered towards them.

When she lowered the camera again, she turned to him. 'If the cattle can't stay here, and you can't feed them, what are you going to do? Can you sell them?'

An uneasy sigh escaped him. It would be so much easier if she was asking this question out of idle curiosity, but she was a stakeholder in this property now. She owned half of everything—the land, the stock, the buildings—and she hadn't a clue how to care for any of it.

'I could sell the stock,' he admitted. 'Or rather, as joint owners, *we* could sell them.' His swift sideways glance caught the rush of colour to Kate's cheeks, and he wished he could retract that pointed dig about her inheritance. After all, she hadn't asked for half of Radnor. And she'd made it clear that she felt really uncomfortable about her uncle's decision.

To make amends, he tried to explain. 'Actually, I don't have many choices. I could sell the mob now, but it would be much better if I could move them onto fattening country first. They'd be worth a good deal more.'

'How much more?'

'Well.' He dropped his gaze to the ground and kicked roughly at the dry earth. 'They're not in top condition, so I'm not sure what they'd fetch right now, but a well-fattened beast could bring close to a thousand dollars.'

'Good heavens.' Kate's pretty mouth sagged as she stared at him, and he knew she was making quick mental calculations. 'If—if a thousand cattle are worth a thousand dollars each, why that means there's potentially—' she gulped '—there's potentially a million-dollars worth of cattle out there.'

A weird little laugh escaped her, and she shook her head. 'I thought you said you were poor.'

Noah shrugged uneasily. 'Potentially, we have the chance to make good money.' He felt compelled to warn her. 'But I'd only make that much if I can get the stock away onto good grazing country soon. And I don't know how I can manage that.'

'So you have half a million acres, a million dollars worth of cattle, and little or no money in the bank. That's a unique example of asset rich and cash poor.'

'Too true,' he agreed, grimacing.

'But what's stopping you from shifting the cattle onto good grazing country?'

Noah watched his daughter. Beneath her shady hat, Liv looked like a mushroom as she squatted on the ground, searching for perfectly round, smooth stones.

Kate followed his gaze and said softly, 'You have too many responsibilities now, don't you?'

He nodded. 'It's not going to be easy.'

'Can you tell me what's involved in getting the cattle to good grazing country? I seem to remember there were enormous trucks. Road trains, I think Angus called them.'

'Road trains are damned expensive.'

'Right. And you have limited capital.'

He nodded. 'The best option is to walk them.'

'Walk them?'

Noah looked at Kate, saw the way her white teeth chewed at her soft lower lip and, for a moment, all he could think about was how once, long ago, he'd kissed that soft, pretty mouth.

He could remember exactly the soft, warm pressure of her eager young lips, and she'd tasted of...

'I don't understand,' she said.

He blinked. 'Pardon?'

'About walking the cattle.'

Hell. His thoughts had wandered completely off-track. 'It's—eh—called droving.' He tried to cover his confusion with a slanted grin. 'Like in the old days. Men on horseback muster the cattle, and then walk them down the stock routes to the sale yards. They were tough, those old drovers. Never slept in a bed for months at a time. Never saw anything except the rear end of a beast. Best horsemen in the world.'

'Quite a challenge. How many men would you need?'

'At a pinch, two men on horseback could just about handle a mob this size, if there was someone else to bring the spare horses and the truck.'

Kate was still frowning. 'But it would be a very slow journey, wouldn't it?'

'Very slow,' he agreed. 'It would take weeks. And that's why it's not really an option.'

'Now that you have new parental responsibilities.'

'Exactly. I can't just head off for weeks at a stretch.'

Sobered, Kate stood for some time in silence and then she said slowly, thoughtfully, 'Olivia needs *you*. So I don't suppose I'd be any help if I offered to stay on to mind her. She'd still miss you terribly.'

'I wouldn't ask you to do that, Kate. And you're

right. I couldn't possibly abandon her. And I don't expect you to stay on here.'

'No.' Her voice was strange and tight. 'I don't suppose you do.'

Noah looked at Kate sharply. Had he said something to upset her?

'I'm sorry,' he said quickly. 'I've been a very neglectful host. I've been so caught up in my own problems that I haven't asked anything about your situation. I don't know anything about your job, or your life in England. I don't even know how long you plan to stay here.'

Kate dismissed his concern with a wave of her hand. 'I don't expect you to play host. You have far too much on your plate. But, to answer your questions, I wasn't planning to stay very long at all. As for my job?' She shrugged and patted her camera. 'I'm a freelance photographer.'

'A photographer?' Intrigued, he stared at the camera she held.

'Would you like to see the photos I've taken this morning? The camera's digital.'

'Sure. Thanks.'

As she gave him the camera he was aware of how small and neat her hands were. Her fingers were delicate and pale, and tipped by pretty, unpainted pink nails. 'You press this review button,' she told him.

'Right.' With a work-toughened thumb, Noah pressed as directed and was quickly delighted by the images that leapt to life on the small screen. Suddenly, the Channel Country's flat red landscape and brilliant blue sky became a work of art. He clicked on close-up shots of cattle, of Liv crouching, searching for stones, of the dried out waterhole. Every shot revealed Kate's artistic eye.

He continued back and found more photos from this morning, taken at the homestead. Sunlight shining through the petals of a perfect frangipani. Liv, fairy-like, surrounded by a carpet of flowers. The rusted iron wall of the machinery shed. A lone clump of drying grass.

Every image had taken on artistic beauty. Amazed, pleased, he grinned at her. 'You're good. You're better than good.'

'I'm glad you like them.'

'So you're a professional photographer?'

'I used to work for a magazine, but I've branched out on my own.'

'That's brave.'

'I know. My boyfriend warned me I'd be broke inside a year.'

Her boyfriend? Noah was ashamed of the sinking feeling in his stomach as he watched a rosy tide spread over Kate's cheeks. Of course a pretty woman like her would have a boyfriend. She probably had a string of them.

Before he could question Kate further, Liv came running up to them. 'Look, Daddy!' she cried. 'I found a perfect white egg.'

With a triumphant grin she thrust a stone into Noah's hand. It was warm from the sun and perfectly white— a smooth oval, just like an egg.

'Hang on,' called Kate and, with a quick adjustment to the camera settings, she snapped the stone cradled in Noah's dark hand.

'Can I keep it?' Liv pleaded.

'Of course.' He tickled his daughter under the chin and grinned. 'One thing there's no shortage of out here is stones.'

'More stones than you can poke a lens at,' Kate joined in with a laugh.

He grinned at her, and he saw that she was still looking rather pink and flushed. 'I think we've spent enough time in the sun for now. Poor Kate's from England and she's not used to this heat.'

Kate wished it was only the heat that bothered her. On the way back to the homestead she wrestled with her conscience. She'd come here to attend a funeral, nothing more, and now within less than twenty-four hours all she could think about was how much she wanted to stay on at Radnor.

She still didn't understand why Uncle Angus had left her this legacy, but with each minute she spent on Radnor she felt less stunned and more grateful. For some reason that was hard to pin down, she loved Outback Australia. It was one of the world's last frontiers. Life here felt like an adventure.

And then, of course, there was Noah. Forget the attraction she felt—that was an affliction she had to learn to live with. More to the point, she was becoming increasingly aware that Noah carried overwhelming burdens. He could really use her help.

If only she had something practical to offer him. If she was a large-animal vet, or an expert horsewoman, even a nanny, she might have been some use. But what use was a photographer on a cattle property?

On their return to the homestead, washing fluttered from lines stretched between two posts in the back yard.

Noah grinned at her. 'Ellen the housekeeper's back.'

'Is she the same housekeeper I met last time?'

'That's the one.' He lowered his voice as he turned

off the motor. 'I suspect the poor old girl was secretly in love with Angus. She took it very hard when he passed away, but she must be feeling on top of things again.' He smiled suddenly. 'Or perhaps she's heard about you and curiosity's got the better of her. At least she'll take over the cooking.'

Ellen was in her mid-fifties, with greying hair and a cheery smile, and she was one of those warm, friendly country women who have the gift of making strangers feel comfortable the minute they meet.

She welcomed Kate and Olivia like long-lost relatives. 'Lovely to see you again, dearies. Now come on in, both of you, out of that heat. I've already put the kettle on and there's a nice, cold chicken salad ready and waiting.'

When the telephone rang, dusk was lighting the paddocks with a rosy-bronzed glow that was absolutely perfect for photography.

'It's for you,' Noah called to Kate. 'You can take it in the study, if you like.'

The call was from her mother, full of apologies for missing Kate's earlier call. 'Nigel took me out to dinner last night,' she explained.

Nigel Grosvenor was a widower who lived three doors down, and he'd had been courting Kate's mother in an endearingly old-fashioned way for well over a year now.

Kate was genuinely smiling when she asked, 'Did you have a nice evening?'

'It was lovely, dear. But I want to hear about you. Have you been to the funeral?'

She explained what had happened, ending with her surprising news of her uncle's legacy.

'Good heavens. How extraordinary.'

'It is, isn't it?'

Slow seconds ticked by before her mother responded and, when she did speak, her voice sounded very high-pitched and quavery, as if she was close to tears. 'Does this mean you're suddenly very wealthy, Kate?'

'Not exactly. There's been a severe drought here, and I think there are problems with money. It's still being sorted out.'

'I can't imagine what you're going to *do* with half a cattle property in Australia.'

'The mind boggles, doesn't it? I have to work that out with Noah—Noah Carmody. He owns the other half.'

'Oh, yes. I remember Angus named him as his heir. How strange that he changed his mind.' Her mother paused briefly. 'Kate, isn't Noah the young man who turned your head the last time you went down there?'

'Mum, that was nine years ago. I'm over it now. And you know very well that Noah married someone else. He has a daughter.' Despite the niggling guilt aroused by her deception, Kate thought it prudent not to mention Noah's divorce at this moment. He might as well still be married; it made no real difference. 'Anyway,' she added, 'I have Derek now.'

'Yes.' Her mother sounded doubtful. Unfortunately, she'd never been very enthusiastic about Derek. 'Have you heard from him lately, dear?'

'Sure. He's been busy, though. Travelling a bit, for work, I think.'

'Are you sure? I ran into one of your old work-mates— Sarah what's-her-name.'

'Sarah Marsden?'

'Yes. She thought you must have been on holidays in Munich.'

'Munich? Why on earth did she think that?'

'She'd just flown back from a weekend there and she said she saw Derek. In Munich, at one of the festivals.'

Oh, God. Kate felt suddenly ill. What was going on?

She finished the phone call with promises to get back to her mother with more details as soon as she had a definite plan. Then, as she hurried to the far end of the house, she reached into her pocket for her mobile phone, and her hand was shaking as she pressed Derek's number.

He took ages to answer. Kate was mentally preparing to leave a rather icy message when at last she heard his voice. He sounded very sleepy and grumpy.

'I'm sorry, Derek, did I wake you?'

'Yeah.' He yawned noisily into the phone. 'What the hell is the time?'

'I—I'm not sure. But my mum just phoned me from London.' Kate couldn't help sounding chilly. She was sure she'd heard a woman's voice in the background. 'Derek, I can hear German again.' She felt a shaft of white-hot panic. 'Where are you?'

He coughed. 'Actually, sweetheart, I'm in Switzerland.' Hastily, he added, 'It's for work, of course.'

'Of course.' Tears clogged Kate's throat, but she fought them. 'How convenient for you to be sent on business the minute I'm out of the country.'

'Kate.'

'Derek, you're in Munich, aren't you, not Switzerland?'

This was greeted by silence.

'I—I suppose you needed the help of a native German speaker. Preferably female.'

'Don't be like that.'

'She's in bed with you, Derek, isn't she?'

He gave an aggravated sigh, while Kate struggled to hold back her tears.

She pressed her lips tightly together while she waited for Derek to protest that this was nothing more than a holiday fling, that he still loved her. She wouldn't take him back, of course, but it might have helped her ego if he'd grovelled just a little.

But there wasn't going to be any grovelling. Not even an apology. The sad truth that Kate had skilfully avoided was that Derek had never expressed more than lukewarm affection for her.

'I guess I'll be saving on long-distance phone calls from now on, Derek. Goodbye.'

She was proud of how coldly and calmly she said this, but as soon as she disconnected she hurried down the passage to her bedroom. Carefully, she closed the door behind her, then threw herself onto the bed and stifled her sobs with her pillow, and hoped no one in the house could hear her.

Derek was a liar and a low-down cheat. He'd deliberately told her lies—about Birmingham, about Switzerland.

No wonder he'd been so jolly and understanding when she'd needed to hurry off to Australia. She'd handed him the perfect opportunity to sneak away with his other woman. He'd probably been deceiving her for ages—with that new German girl in his office.

The toad. How dared he?

It was only later, when Kate was washing her face, that she realised her tears were an outpouring of anger rather than heartbreak. She stopped splashing and stared at her splotch-faced reflection.

Why wasn't she devastated? A girl who'd just lost her boyfriend should feel completely and inconsolably gutted. But all Kate felt was hurt pride and disappointment that she'd been such a poor judge of character.

And here was a funny thing—money-hungry Derek was going to be enormously upset when he discovered he'd missed a chance to hook up with a woman who owned property equal in area to several English counties.

It was a strangely comforting thought.

Kate looked pale and strained at dinner, and Noah wondered if the heat had taken its toll. Or perhaps she was homesick after talking to her mother. He hoped she felt strong enough to talk about business tonight. He'd had a phone call too—from Alan Davidson—and he and Kate had to make decisions.

He stood on the back veranda, listening to the fading hum of cicadas and the chatter and laughter coming from the kitchen where Kate was helping Ellen with the dishes.

He'd left the veranda lights off to avoid attracting insects, and in the shadows beside him, Flynn, Angus's elderly cattle-dog, settled his arthritic bones into a comfortable sprawl and thumped his tail against the floorboards.

They both missed Angus terribly. Under Angus's fatherly guidance, Noah had grown from a small boy to manhood, learning almost everything Angus had known about life and the ways of the Outback.

Many, many evenings the two of them had sat here, with the dogs for company, content to be quiet and to absorb the sounds of the bush. Noah had always found it a comforting ritual and tonight, for the first time since Angus had died, he began to relax.

But it was dangerous to let go.

Too easily, the memories came flooding back—memories of Angus, and then disturbing memories of Kate, and that other time she'd visited Radnor... When he'd fallen head over heels.

He'd been barely twenty at the time, and despite Angus's warnings he'd been utterly enchanted by Kate, bewitched by her porcelain complexion, her fiery hair, and her pretty, lilting English accent.

Angus had him warned him again.

'I can see how it is, son. You and young Kate only have to look at each other and the bells and whistles start up. But this lass is not for you. Her mother didn't want her to come here in the first place, and she'll be beside herself if her daughter goes home with romantic notions about an Australian cattleman. It's my job to send the girl home safe and sound. Uncontaminated, if you get my drift.'

It had killed Noah to obey.

He'd done his best to avoid Kate, had found all kinds of jobs that kept him away from the homestead. But there'd been an afternoon when Kate had found him in the stables.

'I was hoping you might be here, Noah,' she'd said, all innocent smiles and dimples. 'I wondered if you could take a look at my horse. I'm worried he might have a stone or something nasty in his hoof.'

He'd checked the hoof diligently, and he hadn't been able to find anything wrong. But Kate had been so grateful and serious, and she'd asked such intelligent questions about horses and about Radnor, that somehow they'd ended up leaning against the railing of the horse's stall while they talked on and on, without ever taking their eyes from each other.

Their conversation had flown easily, fed by their eagerness to know each other, but the whole time he'd been distracted by Kate's lips, her eyes, her hair, her skin. Kate had told him how much she loved this place. Then she'd stopped talking and dropped her gaze. She'd folded her arms on the timber railing and let her chin rest on her hands.

Her shoulder-length hair had swung in a bright arc, framing her face, and her slender body had curved slightly, like the stem of a wildflower. He'd almost groaned aloud with his need to touch her.

He'd spoken her name in a kind of thick-voiced desperation. 'Kate.'

That was all it had taken—her name—and she'd turned, and her beautiful eyes had widened, her lips parted...her arms left the railing, and...

It just...

Happened.

In a super-heated second, she'd been in his arms and he'd been kissing her, drinking her, inhaling her, embracing her, touching her soft, soft skin with trembling fingers.

Never before, or since, had he experienced anything close to the blazing passion of that kiss. Kate had tasted of flowers and honey, and the sweetest temptation ever known to man. And she'd returned his kisses with such heart-stopping eagerness he'd lost all sense of time and place.

He'd wanted to kiss every inch of her and he'd been sinking so fast, anything might have happened if she hadn't taken a step away.

With one step back, she'd gained enough space to haul her shirt over her head, and she'd stood there before him, her breath coming in soft gasps, her green eyes burning and defiant, and she'd been naked from the waist up.

She'd been exquisite. Delicate perfection. As pink and white as the inside of a seashell.

She was seventeen.

And he'd been warned. Several times.

He'd given his word.

Noah had stammered something. God knew what he'd said. An apology and something about Kate's mother and Angus. In turmoil, he'd picked up her shirt from the floor. He could still remember the fabric—soft and white with tiny blue flowers—and there'd been pieces of hay stuck to it. Clumsily, he'd removed the hay, and Kate had begun to cry.

Silently, making no noise at all, she'd cried while he'd undone the buttons that she hadn't bothered to undo, and he'd rearranged the shirt around her shoulders, pulling it forward over her arms. His heart had shattered at the sight of those shiny tears slipping down her cheeks. He'd kissed her forehead, and his throat had burned and ached as he hugged her to him, gently, as if she might break.

For the life of him, he hadn't known what to say. Truth was, he'd been terrified that he might start bawling too.

Eventually he'd mumbled something, probably something lame about having to get back to work, or even worse that he hoped she had a good trip home.

Many times in the months that had followed, he'd cursed himself for not saying anything to ease Kate's embarrassment. If only he'd told her how brave and honest she'd been, and how much he'd admired and applauded her courage. *Loved her for it.*

But perhaps it was best that he'd remained silent. Why add fuel to a prohibited fire? He'd forced himself to walk away from her that day, and he'd left a brief message with another stockman, then ridden hell for leather to the western boundary and had stayed there for a week till Kate had gone home.

'Noah?'

He almost jumped out of his skin when he heard her voice close behind him.

'I was hoping we could talk,' she said as he scrambled to his feet.

In the moonlight she looked ethereal. She was wearing a pale cotton dress and she was slender, pale and touchable.

'Yes, we should talk.' He had to force the words past the sudden logjam in his throat. 'Would you like to go inside, into my study, perhaps?'

'Thank you.' She sounded nervous.

And suddenly, absurdly, he was nervous too.

CHAPTER FIVE

KATE sat in a brown leather chair in the untidy lamplit study, clutching a tumbler of whisky that Noah had given her, waiting while he removed a pile of cattlemen's journals from another chair.

Still holding the journals, he turned abruptly and frowned at her. 'Alan Davidson phoned just before dinner. He's heard from James Calloway.'

'Already?'

Noah nodded. 'Apparently, Calloway's old boys' network has come up trumps. They're confident Liane has a watertight claim for half of my share, and they can push it through the courts as a high priority.'

'So now the pressure's really on?'

His response was a faintly bitter smile.

Kate decided to lay her cards straight on the table. 'I'd like to help you, Noah. And I'm prepared to stay on.'

To her dismay, he frowned at this news. 'There's no need for you to stay. I can manage.'

Ouch. Coming so soon after Derek's low blow, Noah's quick rejection almost flattened her. She felt like a flyweight boxer knocked to the floor by the first punch from a heavyweight. But she had no choice—she had to put up a fight. This might be her only chance to let Noah see how much Radnor meant to her. She needed him to understand that.

He set the journals on the floor and retrieved his whisky glass from a side table, but he didn't take his seat. Instead, he remained standing, towering over Kate, his penetrating grey eyes challenging her. She resisted the urge to lower her gaze, but she wished he didn't look quite so formidable.

'I don't mean to sound inhospitable,' he said, 'but you weren't planning to stay for long, and I don't expect you to alter your plans.'

'But I made those plans before I knew Uncle Angus had left me a share in this property. Surely that changes everything?'

He frowned. 'Angus wouldn't have expected you to make sacrifices.'

Kate sighed. Was Noah being deliberately evasive, or had he simply missed the point that she actually liked it here? 'Is this a roundabout way of telling me that you don't want me to stay?'

'It's not a matter of what I want, Kate.'

She tried again, taking a slightly different tack. 'Look—I don't know if you even remember how I behaved last time I was here. I was a silly schoolgirl, and I'll admit I had a crush on you.'

She didn't dare to look at him, and when he made no comment she hurried on. 'I can put your mind at rest, Noah. I—I've put all that behind me now.'

She chanced a quick glance in Noah's direction. He stood very still, his mouth flattened into a grim line.

'Whether you like it or not, we're already partners,' she said. 'We're in this together.'

His eyes met hers, looked away, met hers again.

Kate went on bravely. 'You want to keep Radnor, which means buying Liane out, but you don't have ready cash. You want to save your cattle, and that means shifting them to better grazing land, but that's too hard to do alone. You want to be a great father, but you're afraid you'll let Olivia down because you have so many other worries and responsibilities. I'm telling you, Noah Carmody, you need help.'

Clearly surprised, he slid slowly into his chair. His long legs stretched in front of him, and he settled his shoulders into the deeply cushioned leather and took a deep swig from his whisky. The soft glow of the lamplight enhanced the rugged lines of his face. His cheekbones, his nose and his mouth looked more wildly attractive than ever.

He smiled slowly. 'You've really thought this through, haven't you?'

'It was the least I could do, now that I'm a shareholder.' Kate wished she didn't sound so defensive, but for the past couple of hours she'd had a choice—to think about Radnor's future, or to think about Derek in Germany. No contest.

Leaning forward, she said, 'I've been trying to understand why Uncle Angus included me in his will. He had to have a good reason.'

Noah shrugged. 'Perhaps he wanted to heal the family rift.'

'That might have been part of it. But I think there was more.' She circled the rim of her whisky tumbler with her finger. 'I admit, I have no idea what he was thinking, but he certainly knew how interested I was in everything about Radnor. We exchanged letters for a few years after my visit.'

Noah nodded. 'I remember. His eyes used to light up when mail arrived with an English postmark.'

Kate blushed as she remembered one particular item that would have arrived at Radnor with an English postmark—the Valentine's card addressed to Noah Carmody. *Oh cringe,* she'd actually been silly enough to sign it.

'The thing is,' she said hurriedly, trying to push that regrettable memory aside, 'I have flexibility as a freelance photographer, so there's no pressure for me to rush back.'

His eyes speared her. 'But what about your boyfriend? Won't he be desperate to have you safely home again?'

Kate's heart fluttered wildly. 'Actually, that—that's all sorted.' She took a swift, fiery gulp of whisky, then set her glass down quickly before Noah saw that she was shaking.

No way would she admit to Noah Carmody that her boyfriend was currently in Munich, in bed with another woman. 'I've spoken to Derek and explained that I might need to stay on here for a bit, and it's—actually—fine.'

Noah's right eyebrow hiked to a sceptical angle, but he didn't comment. Kate hoped to high heaven that he didn't challenge her lie.

'So that's settled,' she said to cover the awkward moment.

Noah didn't answer at first. He sat very still, apparently lost in thought.

'Do you agree, Noah?'

He looked up, eyes narrowed. 'This is very good of you, Kate. Very kind to offer to help. But I'm wondering what you get out of staying on. I would have thought you'd want to try to sell your share, so you could scoot back to England with some ready money.'

Her mouth opened and shut. What *did* she get out of this? A chance to save Radnor? A chance to forget about Derek? A chance to feel that her life was an adventure, rather than a black hole? But how could she explain that to Noah?

'I think it's what Uncle Angus hoped I might do,' she said at last.

Small lines at the corners of Noah's eyes creased as he smiled. 'And I'd say that's as good a reason as any.'

Thank heavens he hadn't quizzed her more deeply. Kate was terrified he might guess that somewhere, buried among all the plausible reasons she'd considered, she'd hidden another reason she didn't want to leave. But, no, she couldn't possibly still be in love with him.

Could she?

Of course not.

Just a little, perhaps?

Surely not?

'OK,' she said, skipping briskly away from that quandary. 'Now, you can tell me all about the cattle drives.'

'Why do you want to know about cattle drives?'

'I thought we might be able to walk your cattle to the better pasture they need.'

Noah swallowed a grin. 'I'm sorry, Kate.' He began to chuckle, and pressed a closed fist to his mouth as he checked his mirth. 'Taking you on a cattle drive is not an option.'

'Why not?'

'I'm sure you're an adaptable girl, but I couldn't turn you into a drover.'

How patronising. Kate could feel her dander rising. He might as well have said straight out that she was a useless English city-girl.

'Don't you need a cook?' she demanded. 'Uncle Angus told me about the mustering camps. You always have someone driving a truck with cooking gear and bedding and things, don't you?'

'We do,' he admitted, and he took another slow sip of whisky. 'But I wouldn't dream of asking Ellen.'

'I could drive a truck. I can cook.'

He didn't answer immediately, but then he said, 'What about Liv? I wouldn't like to leave her here with just Ellen for weeks on end.'

'I—I thought that perhaps Olivia could come too, and I could help her with correspondence lessons.'

Noah's eyes widened. Kate could see a warm gleam stealing into them, and she knew he was picturing the possibilities. With quietly contained excitement, he said, 'I guess I could ring around and check out the areas that still have good grass.'

'We could contact the education department about lessons for Olivia.'

'I could get young Steve Hatton from Mercury Downs to help with the droving.'

His fingers tapped an upbeat tattoo on the leather arm of his chair. 'I'd be worried about trying to walk the cattle all the way from here. There wouldn't be enough feed. But at a pinch, we could afford to take them by road train out of this really dry country into somewhere near Cunnamulla. They've had some rain there and the country's in better shape. There'd be grass on the stock routes and we could walk them the rest of the way into the Roma saleyards.'

'It would be a real adventure,' Kate said. 'I could take photos of the entire trip. Lots of magazines would grab a photo essay of an Outback cattle drive.'

Grinning now, Noah tipped his glass to his lips and downed its contents, and leaned back in his chair with slouching elegance. 'We're getting carried away.'

'Not really. We could do it, Noah.' Kate was feeling more animated by the minute. If she was looking for a way to forget about Derek, what better way than this?

Noah, however, was looking solemn again. 'You have no idea how rough it would be, camping out night after night. No bathroom, no home comforts.'

'But what's the alternative—watching our cattle waste away? Selling them now and not getting a fair price?'

He rose to his feet, jaw belligerent, thumbs hooked behind his belt buckle. 'You wouldn't last the distance. You'd soon get sick of the heat and the dust and the lack of privacy. And you'd have to put in a lot of time with Liv.' He ran a large brown hand over his face and sighed heavily. 'It wouldn't work.'

Dismayed, Kate jumped to her feet. 'Noah.' Reaching out, she pulled his hand away. 'We can make it work. Just think, if we get the cattle to sale in good condition, we'll turn off something like a million dollars.'

Good grief. Had she really said *a million dollars*? Derek had always complained that she couldn't even manage her modest savings account and credit card. Now she was pulling millions of dollars out of thin air.

She looked directly into Noah's bleak grey eyes. 'It will solve your problems. You can pay out Liane without losing Radnor.'

He rubbed his jaw. 'We're a long way off converting our cattle into money in the bank. It could be a disaster in the making.'

'And it could be a huge success.' Her chin lifted defiantly. 'Noah, I can do this.' Her chin inched higher. 'I am not Liane.'

At first, she saw no sign that her words had registered, and Kate felt herself going cold all over. She knew it was silly to feel rejected, but this was like a very loud echo of her departure from Radnor nine years ago.

'I'm sorry,' she said briskly, perhaps too briskly. 'I'm being pushy.'

'Exactly.' He glared at her, and his jaw jutted another notch. 'And you have a steady boyfriend. Surely he would object if he knew you planned to take off with another man for weeks on end?'

'I told you that's—absolutely all—all right.'

Kate wasn't sure if it was her imagination, but there seemed to be something very odd about this. She and Noah were standing inches apart, staring rather breathlessly into each other's eyes, while he wanted to talk about Derek.

She knew that one of them should step away, but for the life of her she couldn't move. This was Noah Carmody. His lips were practically kissing-close, and there was no way she could be the first one to break the spell.

A hectic pulse beat in her throat. Noah's eyes burned into her, and in the silent room seconds stretched into infinity.

She lifted her chin another fraction of an inch, and she knew that Noah sensed it, knew he recognised her hesitant invitation. He didn't back away.

Blood pounded in her ears and her lips parted ever so softly.

His breathing became ragged as he lifted his hand to touch her chin. It was the barest whisper of a caress with the tips of his fingers. A soft gasp escaped her as his fingertips traced a shaky path over her jaw, and she closed her eyes, recklessly pressing her cheek into his palm.

'Kate,' he whispered, and she felt his hand tremble against her skin.

She didn't dare to open her eyes. She was too afraid that at any moment this wonderful magic would stop.

When Noah traced the texture of her lower lip with his thumb, she couldn't hold back a small, needy sigh. She heard his answering groan, and then exactly what she had feared happened. Noah stepped away.

Clear away.

He gave a slow, dazed shake of his head.

Kate couldn't think what to say, and she looked down at her hands and clasped them together.

Noah turned abruptly and walked across to the corner of the room where a large desk stood almost completely obscured by a mess of papers, Manila folders and books. He picked up a fat book, flicked through its pages, set it down again, and made a small, throat-clearing sound. 'If we go on this cattle drive, I can assure you, you'll be quite safe.'

'Oh? That's good to know.' She lifted her hands, flapped them awkwardly. 'But what exactly are you saying? Are you promising to make sure I'm not trampled by a bullock? Chased by a snake?'

His eyes flashed darkly. 'You know exactly what I mean.'

Oh heavens, yes. Kate knew. She would be safe from *him*.

She tried to ignore the frantic pulse in her throat, and managed a small smile.

Apparently Noah was happy that the matter was settled. He visibly relaxed his shoulders, and glanced at his wristwatch. 'It's getting late, and you must be tired. I'm sorry, I completely forgot you're probably still jet-lagged.'

'I am rather sleepy.' It seemed the safe thing to say.

'There's not much more we can discuss tonight,' he said. 'First thing in the morning, I'll ring young Steve at Mercury Downs and find out if he's available. And I'll put through a call to the education department.'

Kate knew this sudden busy chatter was simply Noah's way of covering any lingering awkwardness.

'Right,' she said. 'If that's everything, I'll say goodnight, Noah.'

'Goodnight. I hope you sleep well.'

Annoyed by his retreat into stodgy formality, she picked up her glass and drained the last of it in one fiery gulp.

He held out his hand. 'I'll take that.'

'Thank you.'

Their hands touched briefly and a tremor flashed through her. She looked up and again their eyes met, and for a split second she saw his emotions unmasked and her heart almost stopped.

'Get to bed,' he ordered gruffly.

Her nerves in tatters, Kate hurried to the doorway. Behind her, Noah turned out the light.

CHAPTER SIX

AN IDYLLIC vision lay before Noah. Hundreds of Radnor cattle lumbered majestically down a mile-wide grassy stock-route. Great shiny beasts in a patchwork of grey, red and brown moved at a steady pace, feeding quietly, while Noah and young Steve followed on horseback, eager dogs at their heels.

Grass stretched as far as the eye could see—a miracle after the dry, burnt-out country they'd left back at Radnor.

It was all happening, an impossible dream coming true.

The past ten days had been hectic, crazy, intoxicating.

Radnor had become a veritable hive of bustling activity. Phone calls had flown back and forth. Trips had been made into town to stock up on provisions and school books. Noah had worked late into the night in the machinery shed, giving the four-wheel-drive truck and the horse trailer complete overhauls.

He and Steve, a lanky young fellow of twenty, had spent three full days mustering and yarding the huge mob of cattle. And, once the mob had calmed down, they'd filed up the loading ramp into the road trains that had taken them out of the drought-stricken country into Cunnamulla, ready for droving.

In the Radnor homestead, the kitchen had become a laughter-filled, fragrant, flour-dusted classroom. Kate had seconded Ellen to teach her everything she knew about stock-camp cooking, and whenever Noah had poked his nose in there he'd found Kate, pink cheeked and smiling, up to her elbows in bread dough, wielding a ferocious chopping-knife, or lifting a mouth-watering casserole from the oven.

Liv had been there, too, working at her schoolbooks at one end of the long kitchen table, or 'helping' when the cooking activities had become too enticing. His daughter had never looked so contented.

In any spare moments, Kate had grabbed the chance to practise driving the truck, getting used to the heavier gear shifts and to towing the float that would carry their spare horses.

And now here they were on the track. Noah found it hard to believe that little more than a week ago he'd been weighed down by problems of Himalayan proportions.

Who would have thought that a girl from England could have given him such a shot in the arm? He had to hand it to Kate—her challenge had been the trigger that had knocked him out of his gloom and set this whole exciting venture in motion.

He'd been worried last night—their first night in the bush—hadn't been sure that Kate would cope with sleeping in a tiny tent and having nothing more than a canvas shower-bucket strung in a gidgee tree for bathing. He needn't have worried; as Kate had pointed out once before, she was *not* Liane.

And this morning she had looked confident and happy when she'd set off with Liv in the truck, trailing the horse float behind her. She was going to drive to the far side of Linfield Creek—he'd pointed it out on the map—where they would stop for lunch and to spell the mob in the heat of the day.

Then she would drive on to their campsite. She planned to spend the afternoon supervising Liv's lessons, and then she would run out the electric fence—he'd shown her exactly how big the temporary paddock needed to be—ready for when he and Steve arrived with the cattle.

Everything was working out just fine. Noah could sense that his luck was changing.

Kate's stomach dropped when she saw the creek crossing.

She stopped the truck and stared through the dusty windscreen, horrified by what she saw. The track dipped into a sandy gully, which was scary enough, but then it swooped sharply into a creek filled with water the colour of day-old milky coffee.

Was she really supposed to drive into there?

She reached for the map and checked her position. Damn. There was no getting out of it; this was definitely where she had to cross. She almost swore aloud, then remembered Olivia sitting beside her.

Well… She'd wanted an Outback adventure and now it was starting.

'Stay here for a minute, Liv. I'm going to take a quick walk out there to check how deep that water is.'

A blast of dry heat hit Kate as she stepped down from the air-conditioned truck. She reached for her wide-brimmed hat, tucked her hair under it and made her way down the sandy bank. She looked again at the stretch of murky water and decided to keep her shoes on.

Yuck. She hated the thought of wet, muddy shoes and

socks, but she wasn't taking them off. Who knew what dangers lurked on the creek bottom?

The water was cool at least and, for the first few steps, gravel crunched beneath her boots, but then she reached mud. Kate's stomach tightened. The water was so muddy it was completely opaque, and she had no idea how deep it was.

She suspected she'd been too cocky when she'd assured Noah she would cope. It had been a matter of pride. It was still a matter of pride. She wanted to prove to him that she was tough enough for the Outback. And perhaps, in some obscure, backhand way, she was trying to prove something to Derek too. Or to herself.

But had her pride got in the way of reason? Until a few days ago she had never driven a truck, let alone a truck weighed down with camping equipment while towing a horse trailer. She'd ventured into some pretty tough terrain in Scotland, searching for the perfect wildlife photograph, but she'd never been a great risk-taker.

Cautiously, she kept going. Muddy stones rocked and wobbled beneath her, but the water was still only ankle deep. Perhaps it would be all right. She turned and gave Olivia a cheery wave and continued on.

To her surprise the creek didn't get much deeper. By the time she reached the middle, the level was still only as high as her knees and, although the bottom was silty and studded with rocks, it seemed quite stable. She decided it should be safe enough to cross.

'Piece of cake,' she told Olivia when she got back.

The little girl gave her an encouraging grin and Kate mentally crossed her fingers, turned on the motor and inched the truck down the sloping bank.

Plumes of spray sheered out on either side of them

as they entered the water. Rocks wobbled and slipped beneath the truck's heavy wheels. Fighting an urge to panic, Kate kept steady, slow pressure on the accelerator and the truck—bless it—kept creeping…creeping… inching forward.

'Like driving on the M1,' she joked to Olivia.

'What's the M1?'

'It's a big motorway in England.'

Crunch.

The truck lurched sickeningly and stopped.

Kate cursed. 'Sorry, Liv.'

Olivia seemed unfazed. 'What's happened?'

'I'm not sure. Probably nothing to worry about.' Kate turned on the ignition and the motor roared back to life, and she gently depressed the accelerator.

Nothing moved.

'Come on,' she urged through gritted teeth. She pressed the accelerator a little harder; the engine yelled. The truck's wheels spun and sent up sprays of creek water, but they wouldn't budge.

Once again she tried, accelerating even more boldly this time, and the engine roared and strained. Kate closed her eyes and prayed, but still the truck didn't move.

'Damn!' She thumped the steering wheel and her eyes filled with tears.

'Are we stuck?' asked Olivia.

Kate dragged in a shuddering breath; she knew she would frighten the child if she was weak and wimpy. 'I think we're bogged.' She gulped. 'But don't worry. We're not in any danger.'

'We could wait for Daddy.'

Yes, she could call Noah on the two-way radio and

ask for his assistance, but she had so wanted to pull her weight on this trip, to be of use, not a hindrance.

Now, she was scared she'd given Noah false expectations. Was this all too much for an English city-girl? 'I won't bother your dad,' she said bravely. 'I'll think of something.'

The mob made good progress and reached the creek shortly before noon. Cattle could smell water from a long way off, and Noah knew there was always a chance they could rush. But he'd watered his mob at a bore yesterday, and there'd been good grazing along the track today, so he was quietly confident that they'd be easy to handle.

'Hey, Noah!' Steve called from up ahead. 'Looks like the truck's stuck in the creek.'

Noah's reaction was instant. Digging his heels in hard, he urged his horse into a quick gallop. Swinging out in a wide arc away from the wings of the mob, he sped to the creek.

When he reached the top of the high bank, he reined in for a brief scrutiny of the scene below, and saw the wide riverbed creased by a band of water. The truck and horse float were clearly stuck in the middle, and the first of the cattle were already rumbling forward, lumbering down the slope, eager to get a drink.

He pulled his hat brim lower against the glare, and scanned the far bank, hoping to see Kate and Olivia sitting in the shade of one of the big river red-gums, waiting for him.

No sign of them. Surely they weren't still in the truck?

He urged his horse forward again, hooves striking stones as they flew down the bank. Any minute now the truck would be surrounded by cattle, milling and shoving and making one hell of a racket. Olivia would probably find it exciting, but Kate could be terrified.

Hell. What kind of fool left an inexperienced woman to struggle with a truck and a horse float on her own? What had he been thinking? He should never have let Kate attempt this on her own.

Noah's surefooted horse didn't falter as he entered the water. He caught sight of Kate's white face peering out at him from the truck's window and his heart filled his throat. To his annoyance, he was forced to slow down, to weave his way through the noisy herd.

She wound down her window. 'Hello, there.'

'Don't worry!' he yelled over the bellowing cattle. 'It's OK! I'll get you out of there.'

He'd freed bogged trucks any number of times. It would be harder today without a second vehicle to tow the truck out, but there was a jack in the toolbox, and he should be able to get a few rocks under the back tyres.

'Noah.' Kate's door opened and she leaned out. Her slender legs were splattered with mud all the way up to her cute khaki shorts. 'I'm sorry,' she called.

'No need to apologise. Sit tight. I'll have you out of there in a jiffy.' He circled another bullock and was able to get closer. From his height on the horse, Kate looked small, fragile, and he was hit by a fierce urge to protect her.

'I think I've fixed the wheels,' she said.

'Don't worry. I'll get the jack.'

'I've already jacked up the truck.'

His jaw dropped. 'You've...*what*?' He stared at her

and realised she was actually covered in mud, even had a streak on her nose.

His daughter peeped impishly over Kate's shoulder. 'Hi, Daddy!'

'Hey there, sweetheart.'

Neither Kate nor Liv looked the slightest bit terrified.

'The truck was stuck on two big rocks and the wheels kept spinning, so I found the jack,' Kate said with just a hint of pride in her voice. 'It's that big red thing in the back.'

'That's right.'

'It weighed a ton, but I found the manual—'

'The manual?'

'Yes. I can usually work out how to do things if I can follow written instructions.'

He gave a helpless shake of his head. 'OK, go on.'

'Once I lifted the truck, I wedged rocks under the wheels where the mud was soft. It seemed to work and I was about to get us going again. But I'd taken so long the cattle were already here.'

He couldn't believe a slip of a girl had done such a mammoth job. Brains and beauty—and *guts*!

She brushed a strand of hair from her eyes and left another mud streak on her cheek. 'I was worried the noise of the truck in the water might frighten the cattle, so I thought I'd better wait.'

Noah cast a quick eye over the mob. The bulk of it was coming down the slope now. Soon the creek water and bottom would be churning. 'I don't think you'd have spooked this lot, but you'd better not sit here and let the wheels sink down again. See if you can take the truck forward now.'

Without a murmur, Kate pulled the door shut and

turned on the motor. She flashed him a 'wish-me-luck' grin, and Noah held his breath as the truck inched slowly forward and the horse trailer wobbled behind it.

'That's great. You can accelerate a little harder,' he shouted. 'Just take it out at a nice, steady pace.'

The truck went forward smoothly, spraying water, while he walked his horse beside her.

At the top of the far bank, they stopped. Kate and Olivia climbed out of the truck and Noah dismounted, looping his horse's reins over one arm.

He had to ask. 'Are you sure you were actually bogged?'

Kate's smile of triumph clouded. 'Don't you believe me?'

'Well—I just—find it hard to believe you could handle a truck jack and know what to do.'

Flinging her arm dramatically, she pointed back to the river. 'Do you really think I spent hours struggling in the middle of that muddy water just for fun?'

'I'm sorry, Kate. It's just that it's so damned hard to extract a bogged truck, even when it has four-wheel drive.'

'I know it's damned hard!' For several seconds she glared at him.

'I apologise,' he said again. 'I'm just stunned. Amazed, I guess.'

She let out a small huff, and then suddenly she was grinning and her eyes were shining with pride. 'I did it, Noah. I coped.' She turned to Olivia, and slipped an arm around his daughter's skinny shoulders. 'And I didn't get too upset, did I, Liv?'

'You only sweared three times,' agreed Liv, smiling broadly. 'And we only ate two bars of chocolate.'

Noah couldn't think what to say without waxing

lyrical and embarrassing Kate. She was an amazing girl. He gave her his broadest grin. 'Well done, Kate.'

She turned a pretty shade of pink and he was tempted—terribly tempted—to drop a quick kiss on her mud-streaked cheek.

Actually, her lips were free of mud—and they were pink and inviting and—

'Hey, Noah!' Steve called.

He turned and saw the mob's leaders already out of the creek bed and on their way up the bank. Not a good moment to be standing about like a thickhead, thinking about kissing Kate.

Noah insisted on cooking dinner that evening.

'You've established gender equity on this camp,' he told Kate. 'And you've already done more than your share of hard work today.'

Kate wasn't about to argue with that, and she grabbed the chance to have first shower. The water in the canvas bucket had been warmed by the sun, and when she unscrewed the nozzle she discovered how especially satisfying it was to become clean again after being so very, very dirty.

She changed into a pale green scoop-necked T-shirt and fresh jeans, and she tried, with the help of the tiny mirror in her compact, to check on her appearance. No sign of sunburn, so that was good. She did her best with her hair, towelling it dry and then brushing it in the last of the sun's warmth.

By the time she'd finished, their dinner was simmering on the campfire, and the tent she and Liv slept in was already set up.

Noah was unloading the swags—the bedrolls that he

and Steve would sleep in out in the open. He saw her and grinned. 'I bet you feel better now.'

'Much cleaner, thank you.' Kate felt more than merely cleaner; she felt brilliant. She'd conquered the creek today, she'd enjoyed a lovely warm shower, and now she was basking in the radiance of Noah's smile... Little wonder she was filled with a wonderful sense of wellbeing.

As dusk crept through the bush, taking the sting out of the day and casting soft shadows, she sat on a shelf of rock overlooking the creek and plaited Liv's hair into a fine French braid. They talked girl-talk about hairstyles and clothes, while flocks of bright green budgerigars flashed past, chattering to each other before they disappeared into tree hollows along the creek.

A short distance away, in the makeshift paddock, the cattle had settled down and were grazing quietly, watched by the keen-eyed dogs.

Noah had cooked a stew of beef, carrots and potatoes, along with onions, dried beans and tinned tomatoes. It was surprisingly tasty, and they ate it on the creek bank beside their flickering fire while a full moon rode high above the river gums and turned the water to liquid silver.

Young Steve amused them with tales of his adventures as an apprenticed stockman in the Northern Territory. Everyone laughed and helped themselves to seconds from the cooking pot and Steve, looking up from beneath a fringe of sandy-blond hair, shyly asked Kate to tell them all about England.

'All about England?' she repeated with a startled chuckle. 'Goodness. Let me see.'

She was hunting for something to equal Steve's humorous recounts of Outback adventures when Olivia, full of self-importance, announced loudly, 'Kate's got a boyfriend in England. That's why she can't have Daddy as her boyfriend. She told me.'

Kate's cheeks were suddenly as hot as the campfire's flames. Even though Noah was sitting on the other side of the fire, she hadn't missed the sudden flare in his eyes.

'No one here wants to hear about my boyfriend, Liv.'

Steve was grinning at her. 'You might as well tell us. What's his name?'

'Derek. Derek Jenkins.' She felt ill just saying his name. She hadn't realised how very quickly her opinion of him had deteriorated. And she felt terrible about lying, but it was better to keep up the charade of a boyfriend than to confess the humiliating truth to this trio.

'What does this Derek guy do?' prompted Steve.

Oh, man. They weren't going to make this easy, were they? 'He's in finance. He works for a bank.'

Olivia looked impressed. 'Does that mean he has lots of money?'

'Liv,' Noah warned. 'That's not a polite question.'

'Derek looks after other people's money,' Kate explained for Liv's benefit.

She could feel Noah's gaze, from the other side of the fire, fixed on her intently.

'Derek should be able to give you sound financial advice,' he said in a quiet, faintly amused drawl.

'Perhaps.'

Desperately, she tried to think of a way to change the subject, but Noah showed no mercy. 'Have you consulted Derek about your new business interests?'

'Not yet.' Tension rose inside her, like steam in a pressure cooker. She jumped to her feet. 'How about I wash up now? It's only fair. You did all the cooking, Noah.'

Perhaps he was as relieved to change the subject as she was, for he rose quickly. 'I'll help you with the hot water.'

With his customary economy of movement, he hooked a long piece of wire through the handle of a billy can of water and lifted it away from the edge of the fire.

He had already fixed a light above the washing-up dish—a purple plastic bowl set on a folding table over by the truck. Moths fluttered desperately about their heads as he poured the hot water. 'You should add cold water to cool this down,' he said, pointing to a bucket ready on the ground beside them.

Still tense from lying about Derek, Kate was in no mood for a lecture on how to wash dishes. 'I like really hot water,' she snapped. 'It cuts the grease.'

He gave a brief shrug and turned back to the campfire, and Kate plonked her right hand into the water.

It was scalding.

'Ouch!' She couldn't help flinching and whipping her hand out again.

Noah was beside her in a flash. Without a word, he grabbed her wrist, pulled her sideways and plunged her fingers into the bucket of cold water on the ground. Her breasts were pressed against his hard thigh, but she was too grateful for the cool water on her skin to worry.

'Keep your hand in here,' he said, pushing her fingers lower. 'I should have warned you. This isn't like hot water from a tap. Smouldering campfires can radiate a lot of heat.'

Under the circumstances it was ridiculous that his touch should send tremors up Kate's arm. Eventually, he lifted her hand out of the water and he held it in both his hands, frowning as he turned it over gently and examined her reddened fingertips.

Get FREE BOOKS and a FREE GIFT when you play the...

LAS VEGAS GAME

Just scratch off the gold box with a coin. Then check below to see the gifts you get!

YES! I have scratched off the gold box. Please send me my **2 FREE BOOKS** and **FREE GIFT** for which I qualify. I understand that I am under no obligation to purchase any books as explained on the back of this card.

▶ DETACH AND MAIL CARD TODAY! ▶

7	7	7	**Worth TWO FREE BOOKS plus 2 FREE Gifts!**
🍒	🍒	🍒	**Worth TWO FREE BOOKS!**
🔔	🔔	♣	**TRY AGAIN!**

www.eHarlequin.com

Offer limited to one per household and not valid to current subscribers of Harlequin® Romance books. All orders subject to approval.

Her hand looked so small and pale against the darkness and largeness of his.

He asked, 'Does your skin sting?'

'Not much. The cold water helped.'

His serious grey eyes searched her face and then, even more gently, he touched the tip of his forefinger to the tip of hers. 'How's that?'

'Fine.'

He did the same to the next finger. 'How about now?'

'It's OK,' she whispered breathlessly. 'Thank you.'

For a moment there, she wondered if Noah was actually flirting, if he was going to kiss her fingers, and she almost closed her eyes in anticipation. She imagined his lips lingering on her fingers, kissing the palm of her hand and running kisses up her arm, like the hero of an old-fashioned romance.

She was in danger of hyperventilating when Noah released her hand and a moth flew into her face.

Shaken, feeling exceedingly silly, she curled her fingers against her stomach. Why, oh why, was she so painfully susceptible to this man's attractiveness?

What had happened to her common sense? Last time she'd made a fool of herself over Noah, it had taken her years to recover. And now, she'd received another painful lesson from Derek. Her ego couldn't withstand another round of humiliation.

As she lifted the cold water, added it to the hot and began the washing up, she told herself it was pointless to expect anything but friendship from Noah. She might as well wish for the moon. Romance was the last thing on his mind.

The poor man was still getting over his divorce, and he had a daughter to worry about.

As soon as these cattle were safely delivered, he would thank Kate for her help, then expect her to retire gracefully and discreetly out of his life. On the first plane back to England.

Close to midnight, Noah stalked the perimeter of the electric fence, checking that all was well with the mob. The cattle seemed peaceful enough, which was more than he could say for himself.

'Troubled' was the word that sprang to mind.

He hooked his thumbs through the belt loops of his jeans and tipped his head back so he could see the full moon almost directly overhead. If Liv was with him now, instead of tucked up safely in the tent with Kate, he'd point out the man in the moon. That silvery old guy looked as if he was grinning tonight, no doubt having a ripe old chuckle over Noah's predicament.

He kicked at a tuft of grass, and a grazing bullock lifted its head in quiet annoyance. He sighed, walked on, tussling with his problem.

Kate.

Yeah…Kate was his problem.

Her idea that the two of them could work together as partners was all very well in theory, but the reality was something else. Living with Kate and working with her, day in day out, was totally impractical—as untenable as Alan Davidson's hare-brained joke about a marriage of convenience.

Twice now, Noah had almost kissed her—no, three times, counting that first time back in the study at Radnor.

In fact, while he was supposed to be concentrating on getting his cattle safely to Roma, *not* kissing Kate had become his number one priority.

Why was he finding it so damned difficult to keep his distance?

Anyone could see she had deep feelings for this Derek chap. She'd gone all quiet and sad when Liv had brought up his name tonight, as if she really missed him.

The crazy thing was that when Kate had looked like that—staring wistfully into the fire—all Noah had been able to think about was how much *he* wanted her. And that made no sense at all. He had no room for another woman in his life now. He didn't need another woman.

What he needed, more than anything, was time. Time to adjust to losing Angus. Time with Liv, to learn to be the father she needed. Time to do everything else that was needed to save Radnor.

Flirting with Kate Brodie was not an option. And anyway, even if she had been free, what had he to offer her? He was still smarting from the battle scars left by his marriage.

He reached the end of the fence line, turned towards the creek and let out an uneasy sigh. Was there light at the end of the tunnel? Would he ever feel really happy again? Every time he thought about Angus he felt a slug of loneliness. And whenever he thought about the high-conflict zone that had been his married life he cringed.

He'd done his level best to shield Liv from the worst of the open hostility, and now he wanted a clean slate for both of them—uninterrupted time to be with his daughter, the two of them healing together, sharing happy times and a peaceful life in the Outback.

Rekindling nostalgia for one unforgettable kiss that had happened way back in his dim, distant past was a waste of head space. Anyway, Kate had a boyfriend.

What else had he expected—that she was still carrying a torch for him after all this time? *Dream on.*

Time for a reality check. Kate Brodie might present all kinds of tempting and pretty distractions. And she might be hard working, gutsy and uncomplaining. She might be fabulous with Liv.

But she was most definitely not available.

And, for that matter, neither was he.

His life was already as complicated as a television soap-opera. The last thing he wanted, needed, or desired was the distraction of another woman.

CHAPTER SEVEN

IF KATE discounted the fact that Noah always seemed to be frowning at her, the next few days were smooth sailing. She was starting to settle in to her new lifestyle. She felt confident driving the truck now. She could build a campfire quickly, and she knew how to check that it was properly out before they moved on.

She had cooked corned beef with white-onion sauce, which was apparently a favourite with men in the bush, and she'd been rewarded with high praise.

'You should enter this recipe in the Jindabilla Show,' Steve had told her.

Noah had simply smiled and asked for a second helping.

Liv seemed to enjoy their sessions with the schoolbooks. Remembering her own childhood struggles with multiplication and division, Kate tried to make the lessons fun, which wasn't a huge challenge when there were leaves or gum nuts or small stones on hand as teacher's aids.

Although Noah was remote and cool with Kate, he seemed happy with the cattle's progress. He studied the map of the stock routes carefully, calculating the distance between bores and working out the best routes, then ringing ahead to warn station owners that they'd be passing through.

Steve filled in important gaps in Noah's scant conversation. He told Kate that the cattle walked about ten kilometres a day.

'But you can't let them go more than three days without a drink.'

'Don't they need water every day?' Kate asked, surprised.

Steve shook his head. 'Noah makes sure they're watered at least every second day. And he tries to find water that's fenced off, so the mob can be contained.'

He told her that the big danger was getting Radnor cattle mixed with the cattle from the properties they passed through. If there was a mix up, they would have to stop and muster out any cattle that didn't have the Radnor brand—a time-consuming delay they could do without.

Kate's one wish was that she could see more of this droving. It wasn't that she didn't enjoy Liv's company— the little girl was lively and imaginative. She was a normal kid, with occasional moments of petulance, but she was surprisingly well-behaved considering she'd recently been through her parents' divorce.

But, although Kate knew she'd been given an important role in looking after the truck, the horse float and the running of the stock-camp, she would have loved to be out with the men on horseback, driving the huge great mass of cattle beneath a brilliant blue sky.

And, of course, she would have loved more chances to watch Noah at work. He did everything so well. When a beast made a break from the mob, he was on the spot to shoulder it back in to where it belonged. And when he was on horseback he looked completely different and happy. He smiled a lot, his white teeth flashing in his suntanned face.

It bothered her that he couldn't look like that all the time.

Just before twilight, a few evenings later, she was leaning on a fence railing with Steve, watching Liv and Noah taking two horses for a canter.

'Can you ride a horse?' Steve asked.

'I rode when I was out here nine years ago,' she told him. 'And I've been riding in England once or twice, but nothing very adventurous.' She rested her chin on her folded hands and watched Noah's happy grin as he cheered Liv on.

Then Liv urged her horse into a gallop. 'Look at that! She's so little, but she looks unafraid and at home on that great big horse.'

'Why don't you have a go?'

Kate turned and stared at him. 'At riding a horse?'

He laughed. 'Unless you'd rather ride a bull?'

She sent him a smiling eye-roll. She was getting used to Steve's teasing, and rather enjoyed it. His friendly jibes were a welcome counterbalance to Noah's remote formality.

She glanced back to the horses tethered in a shady grove of eucalypts, their dark flanks gleaming in the dappled light like watered silk. 'I haven't ridden for ages. I'd need a very gentle horse.'

'You could take Missy. She's quiet.'

Her gaze shifted to Noah who was at the far end of the paddock, supervising Liv.

'Noah won't mind,' Steve said, watching Kate closely.

'I guess you should know.'

'You're not scared of him, are you?'

'Of Noah?' Kate forced a laugh that, even to her ears, sounded far too brittle. 'Why would I be scared of Noah?'

Steve shrugged. 'Beats me.' He tipped his akubra further back on his head and fixed her with his very striking, cornflower-blue gaze. 'Just for the record, Kate, Noah Carmody is the straightest, the most fair-dinkum, all-round good guy I know. He's the best in the district.'

'Your hero, in other words?'

After a beat, Steve said with surprising solemnity, 'I reckon he must be.'

Kate nodded. 'That's nice. And, just for the record, Steve, I am *not* scared of him.' She smiled sweetly. 'So, why don't you help me to get on this horse?'

He grinned. 'Come and we'll saddle her.'

Everything was fine until Kate was about to mount Missy. Just at that moment, Noah appeared, leading Liv on her horse.

'What's happening?' he asked tersely, looking first at Kate and then Steve.

Instantly defensive, Kate lifted her chin. 'I'm taking Missy for a ride.'

His frown deepened.

'I know how to ride, Noah. Don't you remember? Uncle Angus taught me.' She turned her back to him and prepared to mount. *Oh, help.* Suddenly Missy's back looked more than seven feet off the ground. How would she ever get her leg up and over there?

'Here you go,' said Steve encouragingly, and he threw the reins over Missy's back and held the stirrup for Kate.

If only Noah wasn't watching.

Kate put her foot in the stirrup and thought: *Liv makes this look easy. Surely I can do it?*

'OK,' said Steve calmly. 'Get a grip on the wither. Push up and swing your leg over. Nice and steady does it. Now…*up*!'

Kate tried. She really tried, but she got her leg half the distance when she completely lost her nerve.

'I can't,' she whispered to Steve, and she sent a hasty glance over her shoulder to Noah, who was watching her with a darkly narrowed gaze.

She couldn't let him get the better of her. She had to do this. She imagined how fabulous it would be to ride out on the plain, following the mob like the men.

'Come on, Kate,' Liv called from behind her. 'It's easy.'

This was her last chance. If she didn't make it this time, she would *never* get up there. She would be confined to driving the truck for ever.

Once more, Kate pressed her left foot into the stirrup and pushed off with her right foot. She went up in the air and her right leg swung over Missy and, before she knew it, she was in the saddle.

Slightly dazed, she looked down at Steve as he handed her the reins. He was grinning up at her. She glanced across to Liv, who was grinning, too, and to Noah who was not grinning.

But there was a hint of a smile in his eyes.

'OK, she's all yours.'

She gave Missy the gentlest squeeze with her legs and suddenly the horse was moving forward down the cleared stock-route. Kate felt a fleeting moment's fear, but then her uncle's instructions came flooding back: *keep your heels down, lass. Back straight. Posture is very important.*

Her nerves settled and she looked up at the sky, at the bush tinted with coppery gold by the late-afternoon sun.

Everything looked exciting and different from the back of a horse.

More confident now, she squeezed Missy's flanks again, and suddenly they were cantering. At first, she thought she was going to be bumped straight out of the saddle, but then she remembered to lift her bottom slightly and the bumping eased. Now, with the wind in her hair and the thudding hooves beneath her, she felt, at last, like a proper Outback woman.

Perhaps now Noah would show more interest.

That evening, as they polished off Kate's freshly baked dessert of damper and strawberry jam, Liv asked, 'What day is it today?'

'Tuesday?' suggested Steve. 'No, hang on. I think it's Monday. Tomorrow's Tuesday.'

Kate and Noah nodded their agreement.

'What's the date?' asked Liv.

'November the ninth,' Kate told her. 'Why?'

'It's my birthday tomorrow.' The little girl giggled. 'Last year I was counting sleeps till my birthday for weeks 'n' weeks. And this year I almost forgot.'

Eyes shining, she snuggled up to Noah. 'You wouldn't forget, would you, Daddy?'

Noah's throat was working overtime. Kate watched a muscle jerk in his cheek.

'How could I forget my little girl's birthday?' He sounded utterly convincing as he dropped a kiss on his daughter's head and gave her shoulders a fatherly squeeze.

But Kate saw the look of despair in his eyes.

He stood. 'If you've got a big day tomorrow, little girl, it's time for bed.'

For once there wasn't a single protest. Liv bestowed

happy kisses on Kate and Steve and slipped her hand inside her father's. "Night everyone. Only one sleep and I'll be eight!"

Crack!

Noah's axe split the gum-tree log neatly in two. He hefted the axe high again and brought it down, striking the timber with all his strength. The axe-head wedged in the wood and he wrestled it free, lifted it again, ready to strike and smash the log to pieces.

'Noah?'

Kate's voice reached him in the split second before his axe came smashing down again. 'Stand back!' he roared.

Crack!

The log splintered.

'For heaven's sake, Noah, what are you doing?'

He rounded on her. 'What does it look like I'm doing?'

'Chopping wood, of course. But why? We don't need firewood. Isn't it dangerous in the dark? That torch doesn't throw a very good light.'

Enraged, he flung the axe down. 'Is it really any of your business?'

'I—I don't suppose it is. Except...' She hesitated, then said quickly, 'You're upset, aren't you?'

He wanted to yell at her. Of course he was upset! He'd completely forgotten his daughter's birthday. He'd been so damned focused on his cattle he hadn't given Liv's birthday a thought.

As if the poor kid hadn't been through enough in the past year. And, now that she'd been abandoned by her mother, she looked up to him. Liv *trusted* him, and she needed him to be mother and father. He'd planned to be the perfect father she needed.

Already, he'd let her down.

It was bad enough that *he* knew that, without having to discuss it with Kate.

But there was little point in denying that he was upset. 'I—I guess I was taking some anger out on that log,' he admitted. 'Did I wake you?'

'I hadn't gone to bed.'

She stepped closer and he could see that she was still dressed in her jeans and a navy-blue sweater. The dark clothing made her hands and her face look paler than ever. She was holding a small torch, and something that looked like a folded magazine.

'Liv asleep?' he asked.

'Out like a light.'

He sighed.

Kate took another step closer, moving into the circle of his torchlight, and he saw the pale sheen on her soft complexion, the bright glow on her hair, the starry sparkle in her eyes. 'I don't want you to take this the wrong way, Noah, but I wondered if you have a gift for Liv's birthday?'

He stiffened, hugged his arms tightly across his chest. 'What if I haven't?'

'I thought I might be able to help.'

'How?'

She held out a package wrapped in pages from a magazine.

He stared at it, puzzled.

'I know it doesn't look like much, but I bought a few extra things for Liv to keep as surprises. They're just little things. I imagined there might be some rough moments on the trip, so I had a few things tucked away in case she needed cheering up.'

'That's…' He swallowed. 'That's incredibly thought-ful of you.'

'There's nothing really exciting, just bits and bobs from the Jindabilla general store—clothes for her doll and a little bracelet. A few comic books.'

Noah gave a dazed shake of his head. 'But that's perfect. She'll love them.'

'Here, then.' Kate pressed the package into his hands. 'I'm afraid I can't come up with pretty wrapping paper or sparkly ribbon.'

He smiled. 'I'm sure Liv won't care. It's just being remembered. This will make her day. It's fantastic.' He hesitated. 'Except—'

'Except what?'

'It doesn't feel right, pretending I bought these things.'

'You're her father, Noah. That's the point. Liv's not expecting a present from me.'

'I guess.' He let out his breath in a soft whoosh. He supposed parents got away with Santa Claus every year. This deception wasn't so different. Still… 'I should have remembered.'

'You've had too much on your mind.'

'That's the lamest excuse in the book.'

Kate shrugged. 'It seems perfectly fair to me. Anyway, I'm sure you're not the first father who's needed a reminder about his child's birthday.'

He looked down at the package and saw that Kate had gone to the trouble of finding pictures in the magazine of little girls, of puppies and ducklings, flowers.

'Thanks. Thanks so much, Kate.' It sounded so in-adequate. He smiled at her. 'You've saved my bacon.'

It had become a recurring theme—feeling grateful to Kate, recognising how much he owed her.

As if she'd read his thoughts, she said, 'I'll remember you owe me.' Her eyes shimmered extra brightly.

Her loveliness caught him by the throat. He dragged in a shaky breath, and he might have reached out. He might have thrown caution to the winds and kissed her, but as quickly as she'd arrived she retreated, hurrying away, slipping back into the night. Like the memory of a beautiful dream.

Kate dodged saplings, swiping at tears as she plunged through the darkness, following the dancing beam of her torch.

She'd come so close to making a really, really embarrassing mistake just now. She'd almost thrown herself at Noah.

Again!

You owe me, Noah. How about a kiss?

Genius! It would have been beyond embarrassing if she'd repeated the very same mistake she'd made when she was seventeen. Back then, Noah had kissed her out of pity. How much worse if he'd kissed her now as a favour?

Her foot kicked a tree root and she almost stumbled. She stopped to catch her breath and, as she stood there panting, she assured herself that she'd done the right thing.

Last time, her brazenness had sent Noah off to the back blocks until she was safely out of the country. This time he didn't have the luxury of an escape plan. By running away just now, she'd saved them both from ongoing awkwardness that could taint the rest of the cattle drive.

'I'll have to hand it to you, Kate,' Noah said next evening. 'You pulled off a miracle.'

'Hardly a miracle.'

'Liv's had a fabulous day.'

They'd been lucky. They'd found the perfect site for a birthday tea—a pleasant campsite next to a billabong. Now, after her long and exciting day, Liv was snugly tucked in bed, cuddling her doll dressed in its new clothes.

Steve had volunteered for washing-up duty, leaving Noah and Kate alone, sitting on a wide, smooth, red-gum log and admiring the path the moonlight made across the surface of the billabong.

Kate said, 'Liv's a darling. So easily pleased.'

'You have no idea how grateful I am, Kate. Not just for the gifts you conjured out of thin air. You went above and beyond the call of duty to make sure this day was special.'

'I had fun,' she protested. 'It was only a matter of pancakes for breakfast and a chocolate cake tonight. It wasn't a big deal.'

'A chocolate cake with her name spelled out in jelly beans and birthday candles made from green wattle-twigs. Believe me, for a kid on a droving camp, that's a huge deal. A stroke of genius.'

'Yes, well…I have a perfectionist streak.'

'Ah,' said Noah, softly. 'That explains a lot.'

'Some people might say I'm an overachiever.' In the moonlight she offered him a shy smile. 'But it was worth it to see Liv so happy. She adores you, Noah.'

'Amazing, isn't it? I've done so little to deserve such high regard.'

'Fathers are incredibly important, especially to little girls.'

He turned to her, and smiled so warmly he stole her breath. 'At a guess, I'd say you're speaking from experience.'

'I suppose I am. My father died when I was quite young, but I have very fond memories of him.'

'Tell me about him.'

Her mouth fell open. After their recent stilted, disjointed conversations this invitation to chat was a shock. 'I only have very ordinary little memories.'

'Tell me,' he urged.

'What would you like to know?'

'Anything. Any memory. I can't remember my parents.'

'Not at all?'

He shook his head. 'I have a photo of them, and I have this feeling that I can remember it being taken. But that's all.'

Brimming with sympathy, Kate drew her feet up onto the edge of the log and hugged her knees. 'I can remember waiting for my father to come home from work in the evenings. I used to stand at the front gate, with my knees pressed against the metal rungs, and I'd watch him walk from the station, briefcase in one hand, newspaper tucked under his arm.'

She smiled. 'He always waved the very instant he saw me. That was the signal for me to push the gate open, and I'd squeal and run down the footpath to meet him. And he'd scoop me up high and say—' She paused, suddenly shy.

'What? What did he say?'

'"How's my princess?"'

Noah chuckled.

Encouraged, she went on. 'My father nearly always brought me something, hidden in the depths of his coat pocket. I'd slip my hand inside and feel the silky lining and I'd find a small treat, just for me—a sweet wrapped in shiny paper, or a tiny packet of cards, or a newly sharpened pencil.'

'He sounds terrific.'

'He was. I adored him. The way Liv adores you.'

Noah was silent. Kate watched his profile, so familiar to her. She knew every detail—the way his hair tried to curl around his temple, the shape of his ear, the slant of his mouth, the grainy texture of the skin on his jaw. She tried to imagine how he'd looked when he was very small. She said, 'You must have all kinds of memories of Angus. I'd like to hear about him.'

She half expected that he might refuse. Perhaps he'd conversed long enough for one evening.

But he surprised her. 'I think my favourite memory of Angus is one of my oldest memories. When I was four years old, and it was just after my parents' accident.'

He snapped a twig from the log, tossed it into the dark, moonlit water, and they both watched it float.

'My parents had gone in a light plane to the coast. I think they were going to a wedding, actually. And I was staying with one of the ringers' families. Angus came down to the little cottage. I don't remember him telling us about the accident, but I guess he must have. And then he picked me up in his big, strong arms and carried me up to the big house.'

In the moonlight, she saw Noah's smile. 'Funny, the things that stick with you,' he said. 'I remember the cold night air on my face, and the warmth of Angus's flannelette shirt all around me. And I remember noticing that he didn't smell of cigarettes. He took me into the kitchen. It was winter and there was a fire going, and there were three puppies in the corner. Just weeks old, curled asleep in a basket. Angus told me I could choose one. To have as my own.'

'How lovely.'

Noah's smile grew warmer. 'They were perfect for a lost and grieving little boy.'

'And you chose one?'

'Of course. A fat little blue-speckled ball of fluff. A cattle dog, with silky ears and a white tip on the end of his tail. And I loved Angus instantly, because he let me sleep with the pup tucked in bed with me.'

After a pause, she said, 'I think Angus was always a lot kinder than he liked to let on.'

'No doubt about that. He was a true rough-diamond. A tough old cattleman with blunt manners and a soft heart.'

'Some might say he had a soft head, leaving a girl half his property.'

It wasn't the most diplomatic thing to say. Noah, wisely, didn't comment. Instead, he shifted his position. And the subject. With one foot hitched on the side of the log, he looked out at the water. 'Look—black swans.'

Kate followed his gaze. A pair of swans had come out of the shadows, gliding silently, elegantly, into the moonlight. 'Swan Lake,' she whispered.

'Pity Liv's asleep.'

'Oh, yes. She'd love them.'

They watched in silence as one of the swans lowered its long neck and fished underwater, dark feathers glistening in the moonlight.

Noah said, 'Liv claims that today has been her best birthday ever.'

'I'm so glad she was able to ring Liane.'

'Poor kid would have been cut up if we'd got all the way to the top of that hill and still couldn't pick up a mobile connection.' He let out a heavy sigh. 'At least Liane came up trumps.'

'How do you mean?'

'For once, she didn't upset Liv. She actually said the kinds of things a mother's supposed to say to her daughter on her birthday.'

Kate was shocked into silence.

She remembered when she'd been Liv's age. She would wake early on her birthday mornings and run to her mother's bedroom to sit in the middle of the enormous double bed and open her presents. Her mother would hug her and tell her about the day she was born, and what a sweet little baby she'd been.

Her mother always told her the same story—how her father had cried with happiness when he'd first seen her. And every year Kate would ask her mother the same question: 'Did Daddy say I was cute?'

'Cuter than a bug's ear, my darling.'

Those birthday mornings were stand-out golden memories from her childhood.

Poor little Liv.

She saw the unhappy set of Noah's mouth, and her heart seemed to slip from its moorings.

'Don't worry about Liv,' she said. 'She's very resilient and remarkably well-balanced, considering the upheavals in her recent life.'

He laughed bitterly. '"Upheavals". That's a polite way of putting it.'

Kate wasn't sure how to respond. Discussing Noah's marriage felt like an invasion of his privacy. But it had obviously caused him a great deal of grief, and she wondered if she should come right out and ask if he wanted to talk about it.

As she watched the swans glide into the shadow of an overhanging tree, she said carefully, 'I'm very sorry you've been so unhappy, Noah.'

'It happens.' Abruptly, he got to his feet and looked back towards the camp. 'Looks like Steve's finished the washing up. I think he's hit the sack.'

Kate stood too. So this was it. Their friendly conversation was over.

It was perfectly understandable. Discussing Noah's marriage was moving out of friendship territory. It wasn't nearly as safe as sharing fond memories of their parents.

She followed the direction of his gaze and saw the dull red glow of their campfire, the circle of rocks around the fire, and then the truck. She could see the triangular outline of the small tent where she and Liv slept and, on the ground nearby, the bulky shape of Steve in his swag.

A little further away on a barbed-wire fence clothes-line, the jeans they'd washed out this evening were waiting for tomorrow's sun.

The little scene tugged at Kate's heartstrings. She'd really begun to enjoy this simple, challenging lifestyle. She didn't mind rising at dawn. She loved the early morning calls of magpies and kookaburras and the smell of bread toasting over an open fire.

She'd become used to the simple daily rhythms of breaking camp and moving on, stopping for lunch and to rest the cattle in the heat of the day, and then pushing on to set up another camp.

She knew it couldn't last. Sooner or later, they would reach Roma, the cattle would be sold and she would fly back to England.

She didn't want to think about that. She turned to Noah. 'Goodnight,' she said softly, so softly it was almost a whisper.

To her surprise, his hand clasped her elbow and he leaned in to her and kissed her cheek. 'Thanks for everything, Kate.'

As his lips touched her skin, a sweet shiver rushed over her, and she held her breath, expecting him to step away.

He didn't.

An ache flowered inside her, sweeter and deeper than anything she'd known, a longing stronger than anything she'd believed possible. Without stopping to question the right or wrong of it, she put her arms around his neck and drew his head down to hers.

His arms quickly encircled her, gathering her in. His lips found hers with a thrilling, hungry impatience, and he held her so tightly she could feel the wild beating of his heart.

She wanted to stay here beside the billabong, locked in his arms for ever.

But before their tender intimacy could give way to dangerous passion, Noah lifted away from her.

'Kate…sweet Kate.'

No!

The fierce regret in his voice triggered a storm-burst inside her. Her knees buckled and she fell against him, burying her face in his shirt to hide her tears. How could she have made the same mistake twice? What must Noah think? This was so much like last time. Almost exactly like last time.

His lips brushed her cheek with the gentlest of kisses.

'I'm sorry,' she cried against the solid bulk of his shoulder. 'I know you didn't want—'

'Shh. It was just a kiss.' He cradled her head against him and he held her close.

His fingers were in her hair, sifting strands, his lips

against her forehead, and she felt a shuddering sigh reverberate through the length of his body.

With unhappy prescience, Kate knew what that sigh meant. No matter how much Noah desired her, he could not love her. His heart was in shreds, torn apart by another, and any love he'd been able to salvage belonged to his daughter. He had nothing to spare for an English girl who kept dropping, uninvited, into his life.

She stepped away, and gave a shaky little laugh to show that she'd stopped behaving like a watering pot.

Without another word, Noah took her arm and linked it through his. 'The moon's gone behind the clouds. I can't have you falling over in the dark.'

She felt shaken and thoroughly miserable as he guided her back to the camp, skirting the fallen log that had been their seat.

CHAPTER EIGHT

KATE knew something was wrong as soon as she saw Noah the next afternoon. He strode into the camp, head down, mouth set, and without a word to her or to Liv he went straight to the truck and took out the maps of the stock routes. Crouching in the shade of a mulga bush, he studied them carefully.

Finally, he looked up and his face was a picture of gloom as he shook his head.

'Is there a problem?' Kate asked.

He stood, and tossed the maps back into the glove box. 'The bore's dry. Looks like the pump's rusted out, so I can't even try to fix it.'

A dry bore meant no water for the cattle.

'I was depending on getting water here.' He took his hat off and wiped his perspiring forehead with his shirt sleeve. 'I can't see any hope of finding water until we get to Gidgee Creek, and that's two days away.'

'The cattle can last for three days without water, can't they?' Steve had told her that.

'At a pinch. But there's always a danger they'll rush when they finally catch scent of the water. And, with only the two of us, it's going to be hard to hold them.'

Kate didn't hesitate. 'Can I help?' A few days ago she'd finally convinced Noah that she could take over the lunch-time watch. While the cattle and men had rested, she'd mounted Missy and circled the mob, making sure that none escaped. She'd been thrilled to be allowed to make this small contribution, like a proper member of the droving team. It had become part of her daily routine.

Now, however, Noah shook his head. 'Don't even think about it, Kate. I don't want you anywhere near cattle if there's any chance of a rush. We're talking about a serious stampede. Your job will be to keep the truck and horse-float well out of the way. And keep Liv safe, too.'

'Yes, of course.' Kate looked down at Liv, smiled and ruffled her hair. 'Let's hope it doesn't come to that.'

When Kate reached Gidgee Creek two days later, she followed Noah's instructions and set up the camp well off the main track. She was reading aloud to Liv, when she heard the roll of thunder in the distance.

Her first reaction was to search the sky. It was blue and clear apart from a few fluffy white clouds on the horizon, but she didn't know much about thunderstorms in the Outback. Could they arrive without clouds or rain?

Liv jumped to her feet and stood with her head tilted, listening.

'What do you think that is, Liv?'

The little girl shook her head. 'Maybe the cattle are coming too fast.'

A rush? Kate jumped to her feet and looked again in the direction of the sound. Already a cloud of dust foamed on the horizon.

'Quick,' she told Liv, remembering Noah's instructions. 'We need to get into the truck.'

Already, the thundering hooves were pounding closer. Leaning from the truck, Kate saw a roaring tide of beasts galloping down the track.

Horrified, she watched helplessly. It was like watching a tsunami, a huge wall of water coming closer, and knowing there was nothing she could do to stop it.

The noise was terrible. The ground shook. Slipping her arm around Liv, she couldn't think of one comforting thing to say to the child. She had never imagined a stampede could be so terrifying. She was horrified to think that Noah and Steve were out there somewhere in that terrible fury.

Then suddenly Liv screamed, 'Daddy!'

Kate heard the shotgun crack of a stockwhip and she saw the blur of a figure on horseback flying down the wings of the mob.

'I think that's Steve,' she shouted to Liv. The rider was wirier than Noah.

He was trying to turn the mob, and some of the beasts did appear to veer off as he confronted them, but it was like trying to turn back the ocean.

Be careful, Steve. Please be careful.

Almost obscured by the cloud of dust, Steve galloped on ahead of the tide of cattle. At high speed, he turned bravely, facing the herd with his long stockwhip snaking and cracking. Then, to Kate's horror, his horse stumbled and Steve pitched heavily into the dust.

She and Liv screamed in unison, but a split second later Kate shoved the truck door open and leapt out. The panicking herd would trample Steve where he lay, and she had to help.

But what could she do out there?

She stood, frozen by her horrifying dilemma, and then she saw another flashing shape appear out of the dust cloud.

Noah.

He flew down the flanks of the cattle.

Pressing her fist to her mouth to hold back another scream, she watched Noah's horse thunder up to Steve.

Recklessly, Noah threw himself sideways. In one seamless, astonishing motion he reached down to grab Steve's outstretched arm. The boy, clearly understanding the plan, struggled to his feet and managed to jump just in time for Noah to haul him up like a sack of potatoes.

In a flash, the horse was off again, racing out of the path of the charging front line, while Steve clung to Noah's back, one leg hanging limply.

Swinging around in a wide arc, Noah galloped up to Kate.

'Take him,' he yelled.

She was already there, helping poor Steve to stumble from the horse with a shriek of pain. She had often wondered how she would cope in a crisis. Being bogged in a creek was nothing compared with this potentially life-and-death moment.

While Noah took off again, disappearing into the dust as he chased after the roaring mob, she was surprised to realise that her initial panic had frozen. No doubt later her fear would return, but for now her major focus was Steve. The poor fellow was slumping onto the ground, white-faced.

She knelt beside him and took his hand. 'Where do you hurt most?'

'I think I've busted my leg.' He spoke through

clenched teeth, and he pointed to his right leg where his foot stuck out at a sickening angle.

'What about your back, your neck?'

'Shoulder hurts, but I think it's just bruises.' Bravely, he cracked a crooked grin. 'Reckon I was lucky.'

'I reckon you were, Steve. Now, let's get your boots off.'

That was easier said than done. Steve's right foot and ankle had already started to swell, and Kate had to run for a knife to cut the elastic sides of his fine-leathered boot. 'Sorry,' she murmured as she eased it off, knowing it was agony for him.

As she worked, her mind raced ahead. She would need to splint Steve's leg and treat him for shock, so she had to get the first-aid kit and blankets. 'Now, don't move, while I see what I can find to make you more comfortable.'

She hurried to the truck and she saw Liv staring wide-eyed from the cabin. 'Is Steve going to die, Kate?

'Of course not, darling. He'll be fine.'

Kate hoped this was true. She knew Steve was in terrible pain. He could have internal injuries, too, but she didn't know how to check for them.

When she got back, he was still trying to apologise. 'I've let the boss down, and you too, Kate. Stupid to get hurt.'

'Please, don't worry about a thing. Just take it easy.'

The boy groaned and covered his eyes with a grimy hand.

'You mightn't believe it, but that was my first buster in years. My horse stepped in a pothole and went down in the forequarters. Flipped me straight out of the saddle.'

'There, there... It's not your fault.' Kate tried to sound reassuring. She could see beads of sweat on the boy's brow and he looked paler than ever. He was agitated, talking faster than normal.

And, true to form, he wasn't nearly as concerned about his injuries as he was about the embarrassment of his fall and the disruption it might cause.

She glanced back over her shoulder to the rushing mob and the crisis Noah was facing. How could he possibly handle the mob single-handed?

What if he were hurt too?

I mustn't panic.

For now, she had to concentrate on Steve.

Noah's heart pounded and he gulped sharp breaths of dusty air as he chased the head of the mob. He thanked God that he'd chosen his best stock-horse today. He needed every last ounce of the animal's sure-footed, cattle-wise courage.

When he reached the leaders, he turned his fearless mount straight into the pressing, maddened mob. Stock-whip cracking, he cut out a section of about a hundred beasts and headed them west. He needed to spread the herd along the creek, so they wouldn't pile up and get hurt, or trample each other in their scramble to the water.

As he turned back again to cut out another section, his attention was caught by the sound of a motor. He peered through the pall of dust and saw a trail-bike rider working the mob about a hundred metres away.

Someone had come to help. Probably the owner of the property they were travelling through, attracted by all the noise and dust. Noah sent up quick thanks.

Together, without wasting a single word or signal in greeting, horseman and bike rider worked the mob. The trail bike whined and revved, its rider negotiating fallen logs and banks as skilfully as Noah on his horse, and they went back and forth, turning the cattle and spreading them along the watercourse.

Finally the cattle were dispersed, all of them finding a place to drink.

Finally, they should settle down.

Only when he was confident that at last the worst was over, Noah rode up to his saviour—a sturdy, balding fellow of around forty with a grin as bright and wide as the moon. Noah dismounted and held out his hand. 'Thanks so much, mate. I don't know how this might have ended if you hadn't turned up.'

'I could see you were in a spot of bother.' The stranger shook Noah's hand. 'Brad Jameson.'

'Ah, yes. This is your land we're passing through. Pleased to meet you. Noah Carmody. I'm bringing this mob through from Radnor station.'

'Radnor? I heard that old Angus Harrington passed away.'

'That's right.'

'Sorry to hear that. He was a good mate of my father's.'

Noah nodded, then cast an anxious glance back in the direction of Kate's campsite. 'The young fellow with me came off his horse. I'm a bit worried about him. If you don't mind, I need to get back to see how he's fairing.'

'I'll come with you,' said Brad. 'The homestead's close by. You might need the Flying Doc.'

Noah's concern for Steve mounted as he raced back to the camp. The rush had been bad enough, but for Steve to be thrown in the front of the stampeding mob was unthinkable. Noah had never seen anything like it in all his years working cattle.

He'd had no time to think.

And now, as everything that had happened began to sink in, he realised that he could practice high speed pick-ups from horseback for another six months and never repeat today's lucky fluke.

Poor Steve.

He wouldn't be able to ride now. Noah had known, when he'd dropped the white-faced boy into Kate's waiting arms, that the kid hadn't a hope in hell of mounting up in a day's time. And there was no way Noah could drive a thousand head of cattle into the Roma sale yards on his own. Which meant this could be it…

A disastrous end to their mission.

Fervently praying she was doing the right thing, Kate padded Steve's broken leg with a thin blanket and then splinted it to his good leg. After that, she covered him with another blanket to help prevent shock.

To her relief, Noah pronounced her efforts 'perfect'.

'Steve couldn't have been in better hands,' he told her, with a surprisingly cheerful wink.

Then he put through a phone call to the Flying Doctors, and he and Brad cleared out space in the back of the truck and carefully lifted Steve in.

In keeping with the Outback's reputation for hospitality, Brad insisted that Noah, Kate and Liv spend the night as his family's guests.

'It's no trouble,' he insisted. 'I've already rung Annie, my wife. She has a roast on, so she's popping a few extra spuds in the oven.' He gave them another of his enormous grins. 'And there's an empty cottage you're welcome to use.'

When they turned the final bend in the track, and Kate saw the appealing white-timber homestead surrounded by pretty gardens, she felt as if they were arriving in something like paradise. Tonight, for the first time in what seemed like weeks, they would sleep in proper beds with decent mattresses. They would shower with more than a bucket of warm water and they would sit on chairs and eat at a table.

Steve would be safely in Roma Hospital, and the Radnor cattle would be safely herded into one of Brad Jameson's spare paddocks.

Bliss.

The Jamesons' young daughters, Polly and Meg, were ecstatic when Liv turned up on their doorstep. After the first shy introductions, the three girls quickly thawed.

Polly was very impressed that Liv had been allowed to accompany her father on a cattle drive. Meg wanted to show Liv their new puppies. The little girls disappeared, only to race back minutes later, giggling excitedly and demanding that Liv must sleep in their room.

'I can make up the stretcher bed in the girls' room just as easily as in the cottage,' Annie Jameson said.

The shining delight in Liv's eyes was answer enough.

Kate could hardly wait to indulge in a hot shower. As soon as she'd bidden stoic Steve a teary farewell at the Jamesons' airstrip, she went straight to the truck to collect her gear.

Noah was already there, dragging his swag out of the back.

Kate frowned at him. 'What are you doing? Surely you're not going to sleep in that swag tonight?'

His eyes glittered with a strange light. 'I don't have much option.' Without another word, he hefted the heavy swag onto his shoulder and marched to the cottage.

'Wait, Noah. What are you talking about?'

'Come and see for yourself.'

Puzzled, she followed him into the small timber cottage nestled within a grove of bottlebrush trees. The interior was neat, functional and homely, with old fashioned cream linoleum flooring and pretty floral curtains at the window.

A double bed with a white waffle-weave spread dominated the large room. A small kitchenette took up the far corner and a door led off to the bathroom. Kate looked for another door. 'Is this all there is?'

'This is it.'

'But—' She watched as Noah set his swag on the floor and her pulse went haywire. 'Do the Jamesons think we're married?'

'They obviously assume we're a couple.'

'I—I didn't think to explain to Annie.'

'It's not exactly something you rush to point out when you first meet people, is it? "How do you and, oh, by the way, I'm not sleeping with this woman".' His tone was dry as dust, but his eyes betrayed amusement.

'I suppose the Jamesons saw a man and a woman and a little girl and—'

'Assumed we were a family.'

'Yes.' Thinking aloud, she said, 'But they would be horrified if they knew you were sleeping on the floor, Noah.'

He gave a brief shrug. 'They would, but I won't impose on them further by asking for a separate room.'

'No, we couldn't do that. They've been terribly kind as it is.' Kate set her pack on the floor beside Noah's swag. 'If anyone sleeps on the floor, I should. I haven't been chasing after a stampeding herd.'

'You know I couldn't possibly allow that.'

'But I'm sure you were looking forward to a comfortable night in a proper bed.'

'I'll survive.'

She gave a dramatic sweep of her arm and pointed to the bed. 'Honestly, I don't see why we couldn't share. This is a big bed—queen-size at least.' She knew this proposal would have been a lot simpler if she hadn't recently kissed Noah and then cried all over him. 'We—we could make a barricade of pillows down the centre.'

'Forget it, Kate. I am not getting in there with you.'

Did he have to be quite so cutting? 'I'll sleep so far over on my side of the bed, I'll put a dent in the wall.'

'Now you're being childish.'

'Right.' The word emerged as a tight, angry squeak, which completely destroyed Kate's attempts to hide her agitation. Frantically, she rummaged in her pack, searching for her shampoo and clean clothes.

'Kate?'

Her head snapped up. Noah was slouching elegantly against the kitchen counter, arms folded casually, long legs stretched in front of him. No man had the right to look so divine when covered from head to toe in dust.

He smiled slowly. 'Aren't you forgetting something?'

'What?'

'Isn't there a very important reason why we shouldn't even consider sharing that bed?'

She blushed profusely. 'I—I'm not sure. Is there?'

With an exaggerated version of a sincere, furrow-browed look, Noah shook his head at her. 'Dear me. Don't tell me you've forgotten the minor matter of your boyfriend?'

Oh, help. What must Noah think? How could she have forgotten about Derek—again?

Beneath the pressure of Noah's slow, burning gaze, she felt her cheeks grow hotter and hotter. Hadn't he guessed when she'd kissed him the other night that her feelings for Derek had waned to the point of extinction?

On the other hand, she didn't want Noah to think she was cheap and fickle. If he thought she could two-time Derek, he might also think she'd thrown herself at him simply because he'd been the nearest male on hand. In reality, her secrecy had bothered her ever since that night by the billabong. It had lain uneasily in her chest, like an indigestion pain.

Keeping quiet about Derek might have been justified on the night of the fateful phone call to Munich. But afterwards she'd found it all too convenient to throw up the white lie as a shield to protect herself from embarrassment.

Now, however, she'd run out of excuses. It was time to set the record straight.

Hugging her shampoo and her change of clothes, she cleared her throat. 'Actually—'

'Actually…?' Noah's eyebrows lifted expectantly.

'I—I've broken up with Derek.'

His eyes widened.

'I've been meaning to tell you. I've wanted to tell you for some time. It happened before—' Kate's brave confession was interrupted by a jaunty rat-a-tat-tat on the door.

A flash of annoyance crossed Noah's face, but he opened the door to reveal Brad, grinning broadly.

'Just wanted to make sure you're comfortable and to see if there's anything you need?'

'Everything's wonderful,' Noah told their host politely. 'The cottage is perfect. Very comfortable, thanks.'

Kate prayed that Brad wouldn't come right into the

cottage and see Noah's swag in the corner. She felt suddenly exhausted and she didn't think she could cope with their host's confusion, or the necessary embarrassing explanations.

Brad said, 'Annie asked me to tell you that dinner's only ten minutes away.'

'Right. Thanks.' Noah spoke over his shoulder to Kate. 'You'd better get cracking in the shower, sweetheart.'

Sweetheart? So Noah was going along with this charade? Kate hoped Brad couldn't see her blush.

'I'm heading for the shower now.' Grabbing the folded towel from the end of the bed, she hurried into the bathroom.

Inside, she sank against the door. She could hear the sound of the cottage's front door closing, and then the reassuring silence that meant Brad Jameson had left.

At least that hurdle was over. And she'd cleared another hurdle by telling Noah about Derek.

The last hurdle was still ahead of them—an awkward night alone together.

The thought made her body flash with hot and cold shivers. Her heart pounded.

Calm down, Kate. Calm down.

She didn't really think Noah was going to fall in love with her just because Derek was out of the way. *How pathetic.*

She'd given her boyfriend the boot.

Noah couldn't believe how happy that news made him. His veins were bubbling with joy. He felt like giving three cheers and doing cartwheels—for about five seconds—before cold, cruel common-sense returned.

Truth was, Derek's departure meant one thing and

one thing only: Kate was free. Kate, not Noah. This news didn't change a single detail of his own situation.

He was still a battle-scarred divorcé. He was still a single father with a vulnerable daughter who needed stability and certainty in her life. And he was still a cash-strapped cattleman with a drought-stricken property, living a world away from Kate's home.

As his jubilation settled, he heard the sounds from the next room of the shower turning on. Heaven help him; he could picture the soft roundness of Kate's breasts and butt, her lovely pale skin glistening with water, her bright hair turning dark beneath the shower's spray.

Hell. He'd been fighting off images like that ever since he'd left Radnor. Now, without her boyfriend as a barrier, spending this night alone with Kate was going to be harder than ever.

Perhaps he should give up any pretence at gallantry. Perhaps he should just crawl into bed right alongside her tonight, and...

And completely stuff up her life.

Oh, sure, that would be really smart.

Shoving his hands deep in his pockets, Noah crossed the room to the window and looked out without really seeing the view, while he thought about the kiss beside the billabong.

The memory of it made his body ache. He wanted Kate. So much. But twice now—not once but *twice*, for crying out loud—he had kissed Kate and everything had been beyond fabulous. Until he'd called a halt. And Kate had ended up in tears.

How could he have been so stupid—twice? What kind of monster toyed with the emotions of a lovely girl like Kate? He knew she wasn't the type to cry at the drop of a hat. He was really messing her around.

His own emotions weren't too stable either.

Hell. He only had to touch Kate's hand and he was a lost man. How could he try to pretend that sex with her could ever be just *sex* without strings?

In the bathroom, the shower stopped. Kate would be drying herself with the towel.

Erase that thought right now, man.

Noah gritted his teeth to cut off a sigh. He knew very well that many people would see Kate's lack of a boyfriend and his lack of a wife as a green light for a raging affair.

So why was he holding back?

The answer, he unwillingly conceded, was fear.

His fear of another failed relationship. His fear of being distracted from his important role as Liv's father, and his fear of messing with Liv's emotions. Again. The poor kid loved Kate. She'd be devastated if he started something with Kate that ended in failure.

He couldn't risk it, couldn't do that to Liv.

And his fears extended to Kate, too. How could he possibly be the right man for her? She deserved a man who wasn't weighed down by his past, a man could commit without fear. She deserved a family of her own, and the whole happily-ever-after package.

Slowly, unhappily, these truths settled in Noah's head as if they were engraved on tablets of stone. He turned from the window, collected his things, ready for his turn in the shower, grateful that he'd thought the situation through and had it sorted finally.

Now, at least, he knew how to handle the night ahead. He just had to keep everything straight and fixed in his head. Sex with Kate was out of the question. Anything approaching sex with Kate was out of the question. Thinking about sex with Kate was out of the question.

Bottom line, he had a whole bunch of other problems that demanded his attention—a thousand four-footed problems, to be exact.

CHAPTER NINE

THE DINNER was delicious—a glazed-beef rib roast served with horseradish cream, a bowl of steamed green beans, and a platter of beautifully roasted pumpkin and potatoes.

Kate sipped an excellent Cabernet Sauvignon and decided that living in the Outback brought unexpected bonuses. The people here might work extremely hard, but their challenges and isolation helped them to truly appreciate civilised luxuries other people took for granted.

Not that the dinner conversation focussed on the dark, mellow richness of the wine. Everyone was more concerned with Noah's need to get a thousand head of cattle into Roma without Steve's assistance.

Brad didn't hesitate to state his opinion. 'You'd be crazy to attempt it on your own, Noah. I'm afraid I'm short staffed right now, or I'd willingly give you a hand.'

'You've done more than enough to help already,' Noah insisted. 'It's OK. I'll ring around in the morning. There's sure to be a spare ringer somewhere in the district.'

'I don't like your chances. All the young fellows around here have rushed to make the most of the mining boom. There's been a shortage of rural workers for at least six months now. But try the stock and station agents in Roma. You never know your luck.'

'Or you could accept my help.'

The three adults at the table stared at Kate. Noah's face revealed shock, Brad's looked amused, while Annie's smile shone with admiration.

Noah shook his head. 'That's impossible, Kate. I need you to drive the truck and to look after Liv.'

'Ah, now that's where I can help,' Annie intervened smoothly. 'I'd be happy to have Liv stay with us. Our girls would love her company.'

She was almost drowned out by a chorus of girls' voices. 'Yes, Mummy! Yes, yes!'

Kate could see the consternation in Noah's eyes, but she was almost certain he wasn't too concerned about handing his daughter over to people he barely knew. The Jamesons were old friends of her uncle's. And people in the Outback accepted help from strangers as readily as they offered it.

No; Noah was more likely upset because he couldn't explain to the Jamesons that she was no use to him. She was new to the Outback—a city girl from England. But he couldn't reveal that without exposing the fact that they weren't actually married, that they weren't even a couple.

How silly. She didn't know whether to laugh or cry, but she did neither, because Brad was watching her over the rim of his wine glass.

'You shouldn't have any more problems with the cattle,' he said quietly. 'You'd probably reach Roma in about four days from here. And you won't have any shortage of grass or water from here on.'

Shifting uncomfortably in his seat, Noah toyed with the stem of his glass.

Annie chimed in. 'Honestly, Noah, you should con-sider leaving Olivia with us.'

At the other end of the table, Liv's eyes had almost popped right out of her head. 'Can I stay here, Daddy, and play with the girls and the puppies?'

'We'll see, Liv.' Noah avoided Kate's glance. 'I'm hoping we'll be able to get another man to help us.'

'Of course, it won't be as easy without the truck,' Annie continued, blissfully unaware of the undercur-rents whizzing back and forth across her dining table. 'You wouldn't have your gas fridge, and that would be a nuisance, but you could manage with dried food for a few days. I have plenty to spare. You just add water and boil, and the meals are surprisingly tasty.'

'And I have spare saddle-bags I'd be happy to lend you,' offered Brad.

Noah acknowledged their kindness with a stiff incli-nation of his head. 'That's very generous. Thank you. And I'm sure you're right. The cattle are generally a quiet lot. They were only stirred up today because they'd been too long without water.'

His mouth turned square as he attempted a pained smile. Again, he avoided eye contact with Kate. 'Just the same, I think it's too much pressure on Kate. I'll ring the stock and station agents first thing in the morning.'

Kate insisted on helping in the kitchen after dinner and, by the time she'd finished, Noah had disappeared.

Brad, settled in a cosy armchair in the lounge, looked up from the cattleman's journal he was reading. 'He said something about needing an early night. Can't blame him after, the huge effort he put in today with that mob.'

As Kate said goodnight, she pictured Noah, already

in the cottage preparing for bed, and her skin felt suddenly too tight for her body.

Stomach aflutter, she left the homestead by the back door. A pale river of lemon light spilled down the stairs and across the lawn, reaching almost but not quite to the cottage. Kate's stomach tightened another notch, and nervous tremors rose to fill her chest and her throat.

In front of her, the cottage sat in darkness. Why? Where was Noah? She hurried forward, pushed at the door gently and it opened to reveal a small shaded lamp on the bedside table, shedding just enough light for her to see that the big white bed was still made up, as she'd left it.

And in the corner lay Noah's swag, unrolled and...

Occupied.

Ashamed of her disappointment, Kate crept forward. She could see Noah's dark head and the bronzed satiny curve of his bare shoulder. He was lying very still with his eyes closed. She stole closer and looked down at him, as besotted, confused and surprised as she'd been on the day she'd arrived at Radnor, when she'd found him asleep in the chair on the veranda.

So much had happened since then. She'd inherited a potential fortune, she'd broken up with Derek, and she'd morphed into a capable Outback woman. And yet, when it came to her relationship with this man, almost nothing had changed.

She loved him madly; he was as unreachable as the most distant star.

And yet, there had been moments when Noah had looked at her...No woman ever born could be on the receiving end of such intense masculine interest and not be *aware*.

Kate longed to shake him now, to kiss him, to do

anything to wake him. Tomorrow, he was going to hire a new man and they would be on the track again. Tonight they had privacy. This was their chance to *talk*, at least. Surely he owed her that much?

'Noah,' she whispered.

There was no response. He was exhausted, of course, and after everything that had happened today, and with the huge task that still lay ahead of him, his need for sleep was completely understandable.

Understandable, yes, but oh, so disappointing.

Kate supposed the wine must have made her maudlin, but on a scale of one to a hundred this disappointment felt sub-zero.

She tiptoed through to the bathroom, cleaned her teeth and changed, then climbed into the big white bed and turned out the lamp. In the pitch-black darkness, she lay very still, listening to the silence that went on and on.

Her body was tense and restless and she was sure she'd never get to sleep. She rolled to her left side and then to her right, and the mattress creaked each time.

She sighed heavily. What was she going to do? She was as wired as a ticking time-bomb and she'd never sleep. She decided to try one more time. 'Noah,' she called, quite loudly.

'Yeah?'

Her heart leapt. 'Oh. Did I wake you?'

'I'm awake now. That's what matters. What do you want?'

'I—um—are you sure you're comfortable down there?'

'Yes, Kate. Snug as a bug.' He yawned theatrically.

'I—I know you're terribly tired, but I was hoping we might talk for a bit.'

'What about?'

'The things we never talk about.'

For a moment, she thought he might laugh at her, or growl, but he did neither. 'All right,' he responded with surprising cordiality. 'Let's talk about this boyfriend of yours.'

It wasn't quite what she'd had in mind.

'W-what do you want to know about Derek?'

'Did you split up before you came out here?'

'No.'

'When?'

'Just before we left Radnor.'

She couldn't see him, but she heard the way he let out his breath on a noisy sigh.

'Is that all you wanted to know?' she asked.

'It wasn't because of me, was it?' An uneasy note had crept into his voice.

'No, Noah. No, of course not.'

'So why'd you break up?'

Here goes nothing. 'Derek was cheating on me.'

Silence.

'I didn't find out till I came to Australia, but it seems that as soon as I was out of the UK he went to Germany with another woman.'

More disconcerting silence.

Then Noah's voice drawled out of the pool of darkness. 'Were you planning to marry him?'

Gulp. 'Derek never—um—asked me to marry him.'

'But if he had asked?' he persisted in that quiet, half-amused way of his.

'I—I might have.'

'You had a lucky escape, then.'

'Yes.'

In the quiet room, Kate could feel a pulse hammering away in her throat.

'Kate?'

'Yes?'

'It's insane to be married to the wrong person.'

Was he referring to his marriage to Liane? He had to be, but Kate was surprised he'd raised that delicate subject now. Then again, there was something very liberating about talking in the dark and not being able to see the other person's reactions.

She hadn't had a conversation like this since her school days, when girl friends had slept over and they'd talked all night long about their secret hopes and fears—mostly centred on boys, of course.

Perhaps this was the opportunity to broach the unbroachable. 'Noah?'

'Yeah?'

'I can't help asking—what went wrong with your marriage?'

He didn't answer, which was rather unfair, she thought. 'I told you about Derek.'

'OK. OK...' There was a rustle of bedding, as if he was getting more comfortable in the swag. 'It's hard to know where to start.'

'The beginning is sometimes a good place.'

'Thanks.' He let out a heavy sigh. 'OK. I met Liane the first time I went to Sydney for a slap-up holiday. Boy from the bush, trying to make a big impression.'

Kate smiled in the darkness. 'I can see you: moleskin trousers riding low. Boots all shiny. Walking with a bit of a swagger.'

There was a snort from the floor. 'Who's telling this story?'

'Sorry.'

'But you're probably right.'

'About the swagger?'

'About the shiny boots.'

She could hear laughter in his voice, and it surprised and delighted her.

'Anyway,' Noah said, 'I went to a party and Liane was there, in this little white top and a tight white skirt, and she looked—'

Like a tart, thought Kate unkindly.

'Like a film star,' said Noah, and then he lapsed into silence.

'Do you still miss her?'

'I don't, Kate.'

She digested this news, felt emboldened to ask more. 'Was Liane always a city girl?'

'Oh, yes. Through and through.'

'So she didn't like Radnor?'

'First time I brought her out to Radnor, we'd just had a brilliant wet season. The place was as green as Ireland—truly looked like a million dollars. Liane thought she was on clover. She really fancied herself as a grazier's wife. Saw herself rolling in money, living in the big house with a housekeeper or two to do most of the work.'

'So everything started happily?'

'Angus was her only problem. From the start, they just didn't hit it off. I thought they'd settle down when they got to know each other.'

Kate wisely held her tongue.

'Problem was, Liane was too used to getting her own way. She and her brother were incredibly spoilt. Their parents seemed almost scared of them, and gave them everything they wanted the minute they opened their mouths.'

'I suppose she didn't adjust well to the hard seasons at Radnor.'

'Exactly. The next wet season failed and the one after that. Life got really tough and Liane— Well, she just gave up. She couldn't stand the heat, the dust, the distance from the city, the loneliness. I thought the baby might help. But Liv's arrival made everything worse.'

'How? Was she sick?'

'Fit as a fiddle. But even healthy babies are a lot of work.'

'What happened?'

'Liane ran home to her mother, so she could be pampered round the clock.'

'Was she gone for long?'

'Six months, the first time.'

'Gosh.' Kate tried to imagine it. 'Noah, that must have been awful. Didn't you see little Liv in all that time?'

'I went to Sydney twice in those first six months, but both times were a nightmare. Liane's mother treated me like a criminal for putting her daughter through such terrible hardship. She kept insisting I should leave the land and look for a job in Sydney.'

'You would have hated it.'

'I know. And by then I was damn sure if I'd given in to Liane, and changed my whole lifestyle to suit her, she would have still wanted more. I would never have kept her happy. Not for long. I'm not sure anyone can.'

'I certainly can't imagine you in the city,' Kate said.

After another stretch of silence, Noah said, 'But her mother had a point. If I'd really loved Liane, I might have tried to live in the city.' He let out a heavy sigh. 'Thing is, love's a very easy word to say and a hard word to mean.'

Kate's heart skipped a beat. 'Not if you're saying it to the right person.'

He responded with a low sound, somewhere between a sigh and a groan, and she heard the sounds of him rolling over and settling more comfortably in his swag.

'Noah?'

'Mmm?'

'Thanks for telling me.'

'I can't say it was a pleasure.'

'You've been through so much—with the divorce, and the drought and now Angus's death.'

He sighed heavily. 'Not to mention my current lack of sleep.'

'I suppose—'

'Don't suppose, Kate. It's too late. Go to sleep.'

But we haven't talked about us.

Or had Noah, in a roundabout way, already told her what she needed to know? His marriage had left him horribly scarred, and riddled with doubts. He would take a long time to heal, and by then she would be back in England.

There would be no 'us'.

It took ages for Kate to get to sleep, and when she woke the cottage was filled with bright sunlight and Noah, fully dressed and ready for work, was standing beside her bed.

'Have I slept in?'

'No need to panic.' He set a breakfast tray on her bedside table—a pot of tea, a covered plate, toast and marmalade. 'You needed plenty of rest. You're not going to get much over the next few days.'

'Why? What's happening?' She sat up quickly, then she saw Noah's expression, and her stomach lurched in a strange little sideways slide, like a skater slipping on ice. 'Noah, what is it? What's the matter?'

He cleared his throat, and looked at her breakfast tray instead of at her. 'I'm going to need your help to get the cattle into Roma.'

'Oh, is that all? I thought you must have heard terrible news about Steve.'

He smiled faintly, raised his eyes and quickly snatched his gaze away again.

Oh. Her skimpy nightdress was the problem. Kate suppressed a smile as she grabbed at the sheet and pulled it up to her chin.

He said, 'I rang the hospital and Steve's fine. At least, he's as fine as can be expected. Mild concussion, bruised ribs, and a badly broken ankle. But he'll mend after a couple of months.'

'Poor fellow. He's going to hate being out of action for so long.'

'He's already demanding to be let out of hospital.' Noah picked up the teapot from the tray and poured tea into a cup and added a dash of milk and one sugar, just as she liked it. 'Here, start this before it gets cold.'

With one hand keeping the bed sheet in place, she obediently sipped her tea.

Noah said, 'My problem is, I've rung around everywhere and I can't find a replacement for Steve.'

Kate replied with commendable gravity. 'So that means you need me?'

'Yes, Kate. I need you.'

I need you. Three simple words set her insides aglow.

The skin around his eyes crinkled as he smiled. 'I'm not sure you should be looking so happy. If you take this on, you'll be in the saddle for long stretches every day. And we won't have the generator for the electric fence, so we'll have to take shifts at night to watch the cattle.'

'But they're not likely to rush again, are they?'

'I doubt it. I checked on them this morning and they've really settled down. But, even if they're as quiet as church mice, you're going to be stiff and sore and bloody exhausted by the time we get in to Roma.'

Kate didn't care. She didn't care how weary or aching she became. She would be droving with Noah. Truly pulling her weight and proving that she was suited to this way of life, even if Noah was desperate to send her home. She said meekly, 'Noah, I'm your partner, remember? You know I'm willing to help any way I can.'

Bending quickly, he kissed her cheek, and she nearly spilled her tea. But then just as smartly he stepped away, shoved his hands deep in the pockets and stared at something on the far side of the room. 'Can you be ready in an hour?'

Liv was so rapt about her newfound friends that she waved them off quite happily when they set off mid-morning.

Noah kept a weather eye on Kate as well as the cattle. She looked completely at home as she sat straight in the saddle, with her big shady hat crammed low on her head, but he was worried that a full day's droving would be too much for her.

When they stopped at lunch, he unpacked sandwiches and fresh fruit that Annie had given them, and he insisted that Kate rest in the shade while he circled the perimeter of the mob, keeping watch.

He knew Kate was already uncomfortable and by nightfall she would be stiff and sore, and yet so far she hadn't uttered one word of complaint. Gutsy didn't go half way to describing this woman.

Kate watched, intrigued, as Noah set up an ingenious little system to cook their dinner that night. It folded away to almost nothing in his saddlebag, but became a pot on three legs which he stood over the small fire to cook a packet of reconstituted curry and rice.

Kate ate it as she sat with her aching back supported by a gum-tree trunk. 'I can't believe those dried-up chunks turned into real pieces of meat and corn. Oh, look, and there are peas and carrots too.' She was enjoying the meal so much she could almost forget how much her back and her thighs hurt.

Still… She'd survived her first day as a drover and that was what counted. This evening there had been an added bonus—a holding paddock where the cattle could be yarded, which meant she and Noah didn't have to keep vigil all night.

Just as well.

Already, Kate was struggling to stay awake, and she was so stiff and sore she wasn't sure that her legs could carry her across the short patch of ground to her swag.

Resting her head against the smooth tree-trunk, she looked up through the branches to the astonishing purple of the twilight sky. The evening star was already up there, shining whitely. A blanket of clouds, backlit by glorious rose and gold, pressed along the tops of a ridge on the horizon.

'I like the look of those clouds,' she said, yawning. 'I'd love to photograph them, but I'm afraid I'm too tired to bother.'

'I like the look of them, too.' Noah got to his feet and

stood, hands on lean hips, staring at the horizon. 'But for a different reason.'

'Do you think there's rain coming?'

His face broke into a quick grin. 'Best chance I've seen in a long while.'

'Could it reach Radnor?'

'Hard to say.' He came back and crouched beside the fire. 'The rivers in the Channel Country usually depend on rain further north. After a good wet, it takes about six weeks for the water to flow from the Gulf, down through all the creeks and channels. That's what we'll be waiting for.'

'I'm more than happy for it to rain up north,' said Kate. 'But I really hope it holds off here tonight. My first night sleeping out in the open.'

'I'd be surprised if it rains tonight, but you'll be OK. The swags are waterproof.'

She yawned again. 'Actually, I think I'm too tired to care.'

He took her empty plate and she was yawning again, and her eyelids felt as if they'd been filled with lead weights. But when she closed her eyes she could still see the stars and swirling dark patches of cloud.

The next thing she knew she was off the ground. In Noah's arms. Her eyes flashed open. 'What are you doing?'

'Tucking you into your swag. You were sound asleep sitting up.'

Kate was about to protest that she could walk, but with Noah's gorgeous face inches from hers she came to her senses. She had a close-up view of the strong line of his jaw, shadowed by dark stubble. His eyes were almost silver in the fading light. He looked primitive and god-like.

And here she was in his arms, with her head against the solid warmth of his shoulder and the soft cotton of his shirt under her cheek, the hectic beating of his heart so close to hers. She felt secure, safe and warm.

'Here you go.' Noah lowered her onto bedding encased within a waterproof envelope of canvas. 'You're completely worn out.'

Cocooned in warmth, Kate smiled sleepily up at him as he tugged off her boots.

'Sleep tight.' He spoke as gently as he might speak to Liv.

She closed her eyes and felt her aching limbs begin to relax as she nestled into the soft, cosy bedding. Almost immediately, she could feel herself drifting…drifting… She could sleep for a week…for a month…

Where would she be a month from now? Back in England? Oh no, surely not…?

Her eyes blinked open. Noah was still there, kneeling beside her, looking down at her with an expression of such haunting sadness that she had no choice but to close her eyes again. And she kept them closed, holding back scalding tears.

Because now she knew the truth. Noah was definitely going to break her heart. Again.

Noah sat, staring into the glowing coals of their fire. He poked at them with a stick and they responded in a shower of sparks. *That's how I am,* he thought, wretchedly watching the red-hot pinpricks of fiery light. *I'm like a bloody smouldering fire. Any time I get too close to Kate, I practically explode with wanting her.*

Hell. It had nearly killed him last night to keep his distance when she'd come back to the cottage. She had no idea how close he'd been to throwing her onto that bed and ravishing her senseless.

This morning he'd gone through another round of torture when she'd leaned back against the pillows in that delicate scrap of silk she called a nightdress...

With a soft groan, he got up from the fire. A thin moon shone faintly from behind wisps of cloud, and he whistled softly to his dogs. They came quickly, tails wagging.

'Let's check out these cattle,' he said, keeping his voice low so that he didn't wake Kate.

Dogs at his heels, he strolled to the holding yards, shoving his hands deep in his pockets as he scanned the cattle. They were making their usual snuffling snorts and letting out the occasional bellow, but he was satisfied that they were settled. Best news of all, they were in good condition now after spending time in the 'long paddock', as drovers called the grassy stock routes.

With his elbows resting on the top rung of the post-and-rail fence, he looked out over the sea of broad backs and his thoughts winged straight back to Kate.

Until yesterday, he'd used her boyfriend as his first line of defence—had set Derek up in his mind like an electric fence around her.

Out of reach.

Now that barrier was gone.

It would be so easy to give in. Kate was much more than a highly desirable woman. She was a very easy person to be with—calm and friendly, adaptable and cheerful. A good mate. In fact, she was an incredibly convenient package—hard working, part owner of Radnor and brilliant with Liv.

Only this morning, he'd had a conversation along those lines with Liv at the Jamesons'.

She'd cornered him while Kate had still been sleeping. 'Daddy, how come Mrs Jameson thinks you're married to Kate?'

He'd tried to brush the question aside. 'It was just an honest mistake, sweetheart. Annie assumed we're your mum and dad.'

Poor Liv, used to the strange workings of the adult mind, had accepted his clumsy explanation. But then she'd said, 'Would you like to marry Kate?'

He'd been so startled, he'd spluttered, 'W-would you want me to?'

His daughter had smiled and looked almost coy as she shrugged. 'Why not? Kate's lovely.'

Out of the mouths of babes...

Why not? Kate's lovely...

If only life could be that simple. If only he wasn't burdened by past mistakes which left him with an uneasy certainty that he would be exploiting Kate if he made any kind of move on her.

If only he had more to offer her than a jaded view of romance and a lonely little daughter.

It didn't rain during the night, a blessing for which Kate was extremely grateful.

She rose stiffly from the snug depths of her bedroll and saw that Noah was already up, crouched over the fire, toasting bread, heating a tin of baked beans, and boiling the billy for their morning cup of tea.

He smiled, and, even though she was dishevelled and wearing the jeans and T-shirt she'd slept in, there was something in his smile that made her feel womanly and desired.

They ate breakfast, packed up and saddled their

horses, and Noah talked about the cattle, the gathering rain clouds and his plan of attack for the day.

It wasn't until they'd headed off down the stock route, herding the huge mob ahead of them, that Kate had time to think about her sad discovery. Noah wanted her, but he wasn't going to do anything about it.

She was left to gnaw at that bony thought for the rest of the day.

'Noah, I can hear dingoes.'

The sound of Kate's voice brought Noah instantly awake. He sat up and peered into the thick, black pall of the moonless night. A long, mournful howl broke the stillness, followed by the low, tense growls of his cattle dogs.

'Stay there,' he ordered them quietly.

Kate emerged out of the shadows, leading her horse. Having slept for the first half of the night, she was now keeping watch. 'I'm sorry to wake you, but I was worried when I heard the dingoes howling. I didn't know what to do.'

Already, he was pulling his boots on. 'No need to apologise. A pack of dingoes can be a real problem. And a dark night like this doesn't help.'

He flashed his torch towards the mound of saddle bags and located his rifle.

In the torch's beam, Kate's face was white, her eyes wide. 'What are you going to do with that?'

'Protect our cattle—if I have to. You stay here and keep the swag warm. I'll take Missy for a quick circuit and see how the land lies.'

Gratefully, Kate sank onto the swag, pulled the bedding around her shoulders for warmth, and watched Noah head off into the night. She was tired and aching. Still.

Exhaustion, aches and pains had been her constant companions since they'd left the Jamesons', and this last leg of their journey had felt more like slow torture than an exciting adventure. But strangely, the pain and the exhaustion only heightened her sense of achievement— after all, she had to find something to feel good about.

Almost certainly, this would be their last night out on the track. She and Noah were camped at the final bore just outside Roma and, later today, if the cattle met with the approval of the stock inspectors, they would be taken on to the sale yards.

At the end of this day, she would sleep in a motel—no more long hours spent in the saddle, no more nights keeping watch or sleeping on hard ground. Their huge challenge was almost over and, when the cattle were sold, Noah would have the money he needed to pay out Liane.

Apparently, it was then a matter of praying for rain to restore the pasture at Radnor. Once the grass grew back, Noah would restock with young cattle trucked down from the Gulf country in the north.

And Kate's place in that plan involved an occasional international phone-call and dividends paid annually into her bank account. She was going to be rather well off. In England.

Rah, rah, rah!

Admittedly, over the past few days she and Noah had both been too preoccupied with the cattle and too dog-tired to talk about this in much detail. In the evenings, Kate had been almost too tired to eat.

Now, as she sat huddled in the dark, she heard the dingo again. The howl was eerie and menacing, but it seemed further away this time. Finally, she heard the soft clip of horse's hooves signalling Noah's return.

It was so dark that Kate couldn't see him, but she heard the squeak of leather as he swung out of the saddle. Then silence. She could picture him tethering Missy and then she heard the swish-swish of his long legs striding through the grass, and suddenly his tall figure loomed out of the dark and he was sitting beside her.

Her heart gave its usual pathetic lurch.

'All good,' he said. 'I think there's only one dingo. It might have been sniffing around the camp for scraps, but it's heading further away now.'

'Thanks for checking it out for me.' Kate stifled a yawn. 'I hope you can get back to sleep quickly.'

It was her turn to resume the watch. Pushing up with her hands, she began to struggle to her feet, but Noah's hand closed around her wrist.

'No need to rush off,' he said. 'It's gone four o'clock, and it'll be light before long. There's not much point in going back to sleep.'

Kate might have protested, but she was silenced by the warmth of Noah's hand, the electrifying touch of his fingers circling her wrist.

'Sit here for a bit,' he said. 'I'll start up the fire.'

Happy to agree, she held the torch while he selected twigs and branches from the wood pile they'd left beside last night's fire. He worked quickly, fanning the embers with his hat and then adding kindling. In no time bright-orange flames flared and danced, eating up the darkness.

He set a billy can of water to boil and then came and sat beside her again. 'It's going to be crazy and hectic when we get into Roma today,' he said. 'So I wanted to tell you something now, Kate.'

In the firelight's glow, his eyes shimmered, and Kate was very glad she was sitting down.

'I want you to know how very grateful I am.'

Grateful?

Kate wasn't sure what she'd expected him to say, but she couldn't stop a sinking feeling of disappointment.

'Honestly, Kate, I couldn't have done any of this without you. I'm deeply, *deeply* in your debt. Not just because you stepped in after Steve was hurt. You've been fabulous every step of the way. Right from the start.'

Kate knew this was the prelude to goodbye.

The flickering light accentuated the handsome planes of Noah's face. She was going to remember how he looked now for the rest of her life. When she was a little old lady in a nursing home, she would still be able to see Noah's lovely profile in this firelight, the line of his eyebrow, and the small scar on his jaw.

The crazy thing was, he'd become everything to her. Since she was seventeen, he'd been the window through which she'd viewed her life.

But all he could offer her was gratitude.

She'd known this was coming. She mustn't cry. 'I—I wouldn't have missed this adventure for anything, Noah.'

He removed his hand and her wrist felt cold. She sensed rather than saw that he was unbuttoning a pocket in his shirt. 'I've a little gift for you. It's the best I could come up with, given the circumstances. Hold out your hand.'

He pressed something into her palm. A thin pale-green circle; a finely braided bracelet.

'It's just something I made while I was on watch tonight.' There was the hint of a smile in his voice. 'With all this grass around, I couldn't resist.'

'Is this plaited grass? But it's so beautiful, so neat and fine.'

'It's the same kind of plait they use to make stockwhips.' Noah offered her an awkward, lopsided smile. 'I guess it's symbolic, too. We've come all this way looking for grass like this. For cattlemen, grass is more valuable than gold or diamonds.'

Kate bit down hard on her lip to stop herself from saying something she'd regret later. She slipped the bracelet over her wrist and pictured herself again as the little old lady in the nursing home. Would she sleep with a dried and crumbling circle of grass under her pillow?

Noah said, 'Liv and I are going to miss you.'

Here it was. The end. Already he was saying goodbye, and they hadn't even reached Roma. He expected her to return to England without a backward glance.

Her heart began to pound like blows hitting a punching bag and, when a drop of water fell onto her nose, she thought it was a tear. She swiped at her eyes, and was surprised to find they were dry.

Then, as more drops fell, she heard Noah's sudden whoop of laughter.

'Rain! It's rain!' He leapt to his feet and let his head fall back, grinning madly as raindrops landed on his face. Throwing his hands high above his head, he executed a jaunty little sidestep. 'You little beauty!'

His happiness was contagious. In spite of her misery, Kate couldn't help smiling.

Dawn was glimmering pinkly on the horizon. She could smell the earthy tang of rain hitting the dry dust. Beside her, the dogs began to bark, and Noah kept dancing his crazy little jig of excitement. She had never seen him in such high spirits.

'It's been so long!' he cried, grinning happily as he grabbed her hands, pulled her towards him, and swung her around in an erratic, crazy waltz.

Their knees bumped, and then their hips, and rain spattered Kate's face. She didn't care.

'Don't you just love the feel of this rain?' Noah cried. 'Come here!'

Before she quite knew what was happening, Kate was embraced in a great bear-hug and, without warning, Noah was kissing her.

He tasted as fresh and clean as the falling rain, and he smelled faintly of woodsmoke with a hint of dust, which Kate found quite perfect. Rain splashed their hair, their foreheads and shoulders. She closed her eyes, felt the rasp of his beard against her skin and gladly surrendered to his urgent, seeking lips.

The gap between them disappeared as Noah's arms closed more tightly around her. He deepened the kiss and a thunderclap of joy burst in Kate's chest and spread through her body, all the way to her toes.

Perhaps she'd been needlessly anxious. Perhaps she'd misread Noah. Perhaps now, with the coming of rain, everything was going to be all right.

Wrong.

With the coming of rain, the cattle became restless. From behind them a bellow sounded, and then the thudding of hooves, and the kiss was abandoned as Noah and Kate scrambled frantically for their horses.

CHAPTER TEN

WITHIN minutes they were soaked to the skin. Dust turned to mud as Noah and Kate cantered their horses left and right, herding the restless cattle back into the mob.

They couldn't afford further delay while they cooked breakfast, so they quickly packed and filled their pockets with dried fruit to sustain them as they continued on, through the rain, into Roma.

Thousands of hooves churned the stock route into a muddy mess, but at last, by mid-afternoon, they arrived.

At last…

All that was left was a final inspection and the stock would be delivered into the holding yards.

Noah assured Kate that he could manage with the help of men from the yards, so she was given the task of finding a motel. Prudently, she booked separate rooms, and they were quite ordinary, but Kate felt as if she'd entered a palace.

Soft carpet cushioned her toes and her huge queen-size bed had crisp, white, freshly laundered sheets. A flick of the remote brought a television screen to life. And—joy of joys—a big, shiny white bath boasted a row of pretty little bottles filled with shower gel, shampoo, conditioner and aromatherapy oils.

Kate filled the tub high, tipped in generous quantities of jasmine-scented oil and lowered herself into the fragrant warmth. She stayed there until her toes turned frilly.

Afterwards she found the last set of semi-clean clothes in her dusty pack and used the motel's hair drier to style her hair. She grinned at her reflection in the mirror.

Wow! Was that really her? She turned sideways and checked out her butt. No doubt about it; all that horse riding had toned her figure.

Throughout the cattle drive, a wide shady hat had protected her complexion, but there was a fresh crop of freckles on her nose. Nevertheless, her skin had taken on a healthy outdoorsy glow, and her light-auburn locks had never looked so soft and clean and shiny.

She almost gave in to the urge to climb between the lovely white sheets for an afternoon nap, but why waste this improved appearance? Kate had one last night and she needed all the ammunition she could muster. She walked into town to find something flattering to wear to dinner.

They dined in the cosy little restaurant attached to the motel: half a dozen tables, dated decor with shagpile carpet and a fake brick-feature wall, candles in brandy balloons, steak and salad…

The simplest of settings for the simplest of meals… But Kate had already decided that this would be the single most important evening of her life. In the morning, she would either return to Radnor with Noah, or she would go back to England. Tonight, she had make-or-break questions to ask and her entire future happiness hung in the balance.

Noah looked gorgeous in the brand new shirt—white with fine pale-blue stripes—that she'd bought and left in his room as a surprise. And his face lit up with a to-die-

for smile when he saw her new dress—a simple chocolate silk sheath that complemented her autumn colour-
ing, and had the added bonus of a low scooped neckline.

He was in a talkative mood, and as they ate they
talked endlessly, reliving their journey, reminiscing
about Angus, talking about Steve and Liv… And always
Noah's grey gaze was a caressing touch, lingering on
Kate's eyes, her mouth, her arms…her cleavage…

Too soon, way too soon, the meal and the pleasant
conversation came to an end. She and Noah were both
incredibly tired, although neither of them had admitted
it. It was time to retire, to return along the colonnaded
walkway lined with potted ferns, to their separate rooms.

The questions about their future, which Kate hadn't
brought up at dinner for fear of spoiling the lovely
ambience, boiled inside her. She felt as if she would
burst a pressure valve if she didn't speak soon.

Nervously, she asked, 'Would you like tea or coffee
in my room?'

Noah's face became instantly wary.

'I need to talk, Noah. I don't think I'll sleep if we
leave everything up in the air.'

'What's up in the air?'

'We haven't really discussed the future.' Kate slotted
her door key into the lock, then shot a direct look back
at him. 'My future.'

Dismay contorted his face. 'Can't we sort that out
when we get back to Radnor?'

'No.' She'd already decided: if Noah wanted her to
return to England, she wouldn't torture herself by hanging
around in the Outback a second longer than was necessary.

She pushed the door open and went straight inside,
as if she expected him to follow. She turned on lamps

and the room became less generic and more intimate. A hint of her jasmine bath-oils lingered.

'Sit anywhere,' she called over her shoulder as she went through to the small, adjoining bathroom to fill the kettle.

When she returned, she saw that he'd rejected the two small plastic chairs and had made himself at home on the end of her bed. Her legs almost gave way beneath her.

He was leaning back casually, braced by his hands on the bedspread, and his long legs stretched in front of him, crossed at the ankles. His dark hair gleamed in the lamplight, and his crisp new shirt outlined the powerful breadth of his shoulders.

Noah, her gorgeous, gorgeous cattleman.

This morning he'd kissed her in the rain, and she could still feel the warmth of his arms about her, the heady joy of his lips, hungry on hers.

It could happen again now.

Kate was terribly tempted to leap onto the bed. She could have him on his back in five seconds flat. Heat swirled through her as she pictured it. She could already taste Noah, smell him, feel him. Her hands were shaking as she set the kettle on the counter and plugged it in.

The low rumble of the heating jug filled the small room.

Noah cleared his throat. 'What exactly do you want to discuss?'

Defensively, Kate folded her arms across her chest, ready for a showdown. 'I would like to know exactly where I stand.'

He watched her with a cautious, slightly puzzled frown.

She swallowed. 'Are you expecting me to return to England?'

'You want to go back, don't you?'

'Not really.'

In a flash, Noah abandoned his relaxed pose and swung upright, sat stiffly on the edge of the bed. 'You don't want to be stuck in the Outback, Kate. You've had a bit of an adventure, but now you need to get on with your life.'

Slam. Wrong response. How could he be so clueless? 'I told you I've broken up with Derek.'

'Ye—es.' He dragged the word out, making it sound unbelievably cautious.

'So, you know, I'm—I'm—' Frantically, she discarded words like 'free' and 'in love' and hunted for something safer. 'I don't need to race back.'

Noah dropped his gaze to the mustard-toned carpet. 'But surely Derek isn't the only attraction in England? What about your mother? Your job?'

'What about you, Noah?'

His head snapped up.

'Are you going to pretend we aren't the slightest bit attracted to each other?' Kate couldn't believe she'd finally asked that question. She held her breath as she watched Noah's face grow grimmer and grimmer, and she wondered if it was possible to die of embarrassment.

Behind her the kettle came to the boil, but she ignored it.

'When you kissed me this morning, what was that about? Were you simply excited about the rain?'

He groaned softly, then he stood, said slowly, sadly, 'Kate, I'm not the man for you.'

'Isn't that for me to decide?' Her voice quavered tremulously. 'Or are you actually telling me that I'm not the woman for you?'

He looked at her, his eyes dark with pain. 'I guess that's exactly what I'm saying.'

Noah, don't do this. I know that's not true. Be honest.

'And—and do you think it's irrelevant that I love Radnor?'

He shook his head. 'On the contrary. That's a big part of the problem.'

'How?'

'We share Radnor, Kate. We're business partners. But if we—' He came closer and lifted his hand as if he wanted to touch her cheek.

Her heart almost stopped beating.

'You're so lovely, Kate. And this chocolate-silk dress is driving me insane. To be honest, there is nothing in the world I want more than to help you out of it.'

'I—w-wouldn't object,' she said, blushing madly.

His mouth twisted, and with a choked sigh he let his hand drop and he shoved it into his jeans pocket, as if he needed to keep it out of harm's way. He said, 'I think you might object if you knew there was a catch.'

'What catch?'

'The best we could hope for is a brief affair.'

I'll take it, Kate almost told him.

'There's no chance of anything long term,' he said.

'And you know this in advance?'

He nodded solemnly. 'When it comes to my emotions, I'm running on empty, Kate. I seem to have lost faith in my instincts.' He looked down at the carpet again. 'You know what I've been through. When I married Liane, I thought I loved her.' He released a sigh. 'But now I can only feel pity for her, and an emotion so far removed from love it frightens me. I—I don't know what love is any more.'

Kate took a deep breath. 'Well, here's a funny thing, Noah. I was foolish enough to fall in love with you when I was seventeen. And I've never really recovered.'

For one crazy moment, she thought he was going haul

her across the carpet and into his arms. But then he frowned at her, as if he was wrestling with a new problem. Very quietly, he said, 'I don't deserve you, Kate.'

'Love's not about deserving.'

'But it is where you're concerned. Think about it. You've given and given. From the minute you arrived on Radnor, you've been extraordinary. You've looked after Liv, Steve—all of us. I've given you nothing in return.'

She fingered the grass bracelet around her wrist, then, suddenly weary and on the verge of breaking down, she sank onto a plastic chair. 'I may as well confess the whole painful, ugly truth. I've never been able to fall in love with any of my boyfriends. And—and it's because of you, Noah.'

'I should never have kissed you.'

She gave him a weary smile. 'All it took was one kiss—nine years ago. Crazy, isn't it?'

'No, Kate. Not crazy.'

His answer lingered in the air between them, reso-nating with promise, like the first notes of a beautiful song. Kate held her breath as she waited.

'I'm so sorry,' he said inadequately.

So…

There would be no song.

Her mouth trembled as she struggled to ignore the shattering pain inside her. The only way to survive this was to be brave.

'I suppose you can't help it, Noah. You didn't try to make me fall in love with you. It just happened.'

He gave a bewildered shake of his head. 'But I'm not right for you, Kate. Not any more. And it's too late to undo the damage.'

'Is it?'

Two tiny words, trembling with shameless hope.

Noah heard them and fought down his rising panic. He couldn't bear to watch this wonderful, wonderful girl walk out of his life, but what right had he to try to keep her?

He'd thought this through so many times and he'd always come up with the same answer: she needed a man who could love her confidently. Completely. How could he make her understand his fears? His doubts?

'Is it really too late, Noah?' Her face was white.

He swallowed the painful block of ice in his throat. 'I can't give you the kind of promise you need.'

If his marriage had taught him anything, he'd learned that a mad attraction was not love. Right now, he wanted to strip that sexy dress from Kate's pale, softer-than-silk curves, to take her to bed and lose himself in her. But she was too fine a woman to demean with an offer of love that fell short of the mark.

Noah needed to pace, to think, to find the right words to explain all this without hurting her.

The room was too damn small for pacing. He ran an anguished hand over his face, let out a wretched sigh.

Behind him, Kate said, 'I think you'd better go.'

He spun round. She was standing very still with her head high and her shoulders back, like a warrior woman facing up to her fiercest enemy.

Oh, God. All he had to do was tell her now that he loved her and he could make everything right.

It should be so easy. With three simple words...*I love you*...he could banish those dreadful shadows from her eyes. He could make her smile.

He so wanted to see her smile. In the best of all possible worlds, he would wake every day to Kate's sweet, warm smile.

All she asked for was love.

Love. Ever after.

If only he could believe it was possible.

'Noah, I'm very tired. Will you please leave?'

Warrior Woman had crumpled. Kate was white and trembling, clutching the edge of the counter, as if she needed its support.

'But I haven't explained anything properly.'

'You don't need to explain. I understand perfectly.' She pointed to the door. 'Believe me, I've got the message.'

Desperately, he clutched at straws. He couldn't let it end like this. 'Perhaps we could talk this through in the morning?'

'Yes,' Kate said flatly. 'We can talk in the morning. But, for now, goodnight. I need you to go.'

'Darling, it's so good to hear from you at last. Your phone's been out of reach for ages and I've been worried. How are you?'

Kate looked out at the grey rain sweeping across Laguna Bay and squeezed her face muscles in an attempt at a smile. If she was smiling, her voice might sound brighter. 'I'm fine, Mum.'

'Are you sure, Kate? You don't sound fine.'

'Honestly, I'm right as rain. And, speaking of rain, it's pouring all over Queensland, which is really good news, because they've had such a terrible drought.'

'I see. That's nice, dear, but you're babbling, and you only babble when you're upset.'

Kate blinked back tears. 'I'm not upset. Really.' *Liar.* She'd cried so much in the past three days she was afraid she'd caused permanent damage to her tear ducts.

'Have you finished the cattle drive?'

'Yes. It went very well, but I'll tell you all about it when I get home.' Perhaps by then she would be able to mention Noah Carmody's name without another dam burst.

'I can't wait to see you, darling. When will you be back?'

'Next week. I'll be arriving in Heathrow at four o'clock on Wednesday afternoon.'

'Oh, darling, that's lovely. Fantastic, actually. You'll be back in time for our celebrations.'

'What are you celebrating?' Kate had never heard her mother sound so girlish and excited.

'Kate, you'll never believe this. Nigel has asked me to marry him and I've said yes.'

Just in time, Kate clamped her hand over her mouth and stifled her cry of dismay.

'Kate, are you there?'

'Yes, Mum.' Oh, good grief. She couldn't believe she was jealous of her mother. The poor woman had been a widow for such a long time and she really deserved this happiness. 'Wow, that's—fabulous news. I'm so, so happy for you.'

'I was half expecting that you might have news, too, Kate. About your young man.'

'No. No news.' Kate said this in her most decisive 'let's drop it' voice, but her mother was too happy and curious to notice.

'Are you disappointed, darling?'

'No.' *Liar, liar.* 'I had a fabulous time bringing the cattle along the stock routes. It was quite an adventure, you know. I took some amazing photographs, but now I'm ready to come home.'

'So where are you? Back at Radnor?'

'Actually, I'm at Noosa. It's a seaside resort, over on

the coast, and it's beautiful.' She couldn't admit that
she'd run away from Roma, leaving the motel in the
early hours and catching a bus heading east.

'The beaches are just beautiful here, Mum. Of
course, they're not looking their best now with all the
rain. But there's a walk through the national park that
takes you out around the headland. And the shops are
gorgeous. I'm having a break here before I fly home.'

It was more or less the truth. More accurately, Kate
was holed up in Noosa, trying to pull herself together
before she faced the ordeal of returning to England to
pick up the tattered shreds of her life.

Her days were spent walking in the rain, or sitting
and staring at storm-tossed seas while she reminded
herself over and over that this misery was self-induced.
It was the price she had to pay for foolishly falling in
love with Noah Carmody for a second time.

Tourist brochures about Noosa and posters in shop
windows showed how stunningly beautiful this beach
could be when the weather was calm and sunny, but the
recent storms and the angry, desolate waves matched
Kate's mood. She'd spent entire afternoons sitting in
cafés set right at the edge of the sand.

Endlessly, she'd watched the surf seethe and boil
until it finally spent itself on the shore, running up the
beach in thin, lacy frills. She wished she could be like
those waves. If only she could hurl her heartbreak into
the universe, let her despair finally crash on some
distant shore and disperse, getting smaller and smaller
until it was a mere droplet that no longer had the power
to hurt her.

But there was no simple quick fix for her problem.
The process of rebuilding her broken heart for the

second time was going to be as slow and agonising as it had been the first time. Worse, actually, because her feelings for Noah were based on so much more than one kiss. She'd taken his daughter into her heart. She'd joined him in his work…endured his hardships…shared his triumphs. But now she had to put that sorry misadventure behind her.

It would be much easier if she and Noah weren't joint owners of Radnor. That connection was a killer. But Kate was confident she could find lawyers and accountants who'd negotiate a deal which allowed her share of the property to gradually transfer to Noah at a rate he could afford.

In the end, Kate would be a rich woman, and no doubt she would still be working very hard at being happy in England. And Noah, as full owner of the property he loved, would be living his dream.

It was still raining on Tuesday afternoon, Kate's last afternoon in Australia. But despite the dismal outlook, she drank her usual cappuccino at a table on the edge of the beach. Afterwards, she walked back along Hastings Street, stopping at the tiny supermarket to buy a tin of tomato and basil soup and two dinner rolls for her evening meal.

Then she continued on, past fashion shops, trendy art galleries and ice-creameries, to a boardwalk that took her around the headland to Little Cove where her holiday cabin nestled among towering gum-trees.

The fellow in charge of Reception gave her an extra warm smile as she walked through the foyer with her damp shopping bags and dripping umbrella. 'Miss Brodie,' he called. 'I have some lost property for you.'

Kate couldn't think of anything she'd lost. 'Are you sure, Fred?'

He retrieved an envelope from a row of numbered pigeonholes behind him. 'This was handed in while I was on my lunch break.' When he saw Kate's frown, he said, 'It has your name on it, but if there's been a mistake just pop it back and we'll do our best to find the right owner.'

'All right. Thanks.' Still frowning, Kate accepted the envelope. Her name was scrawled in spiky handwriting on the front.

Puzzled, she slipped it into her bag and hurried along the brick path to her cabin, dodging puddles, shiny, wet palm fronds and drooping hibiscus flowers.

Inside, she dumped her shopping on the counter in the kitchenette and pulled the envelope from her bag, slipped her finger beneath the flap and tore it open.

When she looked inside her heart leapt high and hard. She hadn't seen the Valentine's card for almost nine years, but she would have recognised it anywhere. She'd made it herself—a photo of Noah striding through the home paddock, carrying a bridle in one hand, and a saddle on his shoulder, framed by a red heart and pasted onto purple cardboard.

She'd sent this to him when she was eighteen.

Her heart began to pound and her vision blurred. She couldn't believe he'd kept it all this time. Couldn't believe it had reached her now. In Noosa.

Why?

How?

Her hands shook as she opened the card, and she felt a quick flash of embarrassment at the prospect of seeing her name written inside. But there was another surprise!

A circle of dried woven grass.

The bracelet Noah had made for her.

She clapped a hand over her trembling mouth as she remembered how this bracelet had looked the last time she'd seen it—lying forlornly on the bedside table in her motel room in Roma. She'd left it there because she couldn't bear to keep such a painful memento.

Now, here it was.

His gift to her...

And her gift to him.

But where was Noah? How had he found her?

Until this moment, Kate's hasty departure had felt totally reasonable, but now she wasn't so sure. He must have found her. Who else could have handed this in at Reception? Her heart slammed hard in her chest as she rushed to the door of her cabin and scanned the rain-washed gardens, hoping to see him.

Two children in yellow raincoats were running and squealing and stomping in puddles, but otherwise the gardens were empty.

She sank against the door frame. How could she bear this suspense? Fred had been on his lunch break, so he hadn't seen the person who'd delivered the envelope. Even so, he might have heard *something*. She should go back to Reception and ask more questions.

Without stopping to fetch her umbrella or her keys, or to shut the front door, she ran back down the path, and as she rounded the last cabin she almost bumped into a tall figure in a dark waterproof coat.

A jolt of heat flashed through her all the way to her rubber flip-flops.

Noah.

He looked very tall and more than a little damp and

every version of wonderful. And he was smiling at her. 'Kate, I'm so glad I found you.'

She pressed a hand against the thumping in her chest. Her head spun dizzily. 'How *did* you find me?'

'I rang your mother. She was enormously helpful.'

Noah's gaze dropped to the bracelet on her wrist, and the card, and his eyes glowed with heart-stopping warmth.

'You kept the card all this time, Noah.'

'Of course I kept it, but I've been such a fool.' He reached out to touch the bracelet. 'When I saw this and realised you'd gone, I knew I'd made the worst mistake of my life.'

'Is that why you've come all this way?'

'Yes. I was ready to go to England if I had to. We didn't finish our conversation.'

She gave him a teary smile. 'Should we get out of this rain.'

Threading his fingers through hers, he said, 'We can go anywhere you like, as long as you don't disappear again.'

Giant butterflies danced in her stomach as they went back along the path to her cabin. Noah discarded his coat and hung it in the porch.

'You're wet,' he said, as if he'd only just noticed her damp state.

'It doesn't matter.' Nothing mattered if Noah had come to her for all the right reasons.

He was wearing his customary long-sleeved shirt, blue jeans and riding boots and Kate, in a rain-splattered yellow sundress and flip-flops, thought he had never looked more wonderful. Her heart ached as she took in each dear, familiar, handsome detail of his face.

'So you want to finish our conversation?' she said in a voice that trembled.

'I want to start a new conversation.'

Kate held her breath.

'I can't put my feelings into verse the way your lovely card did, but I love you, Kate.' His face broke into a beautiful smile. 'I mean it. Honestly. Even though I rattled on about not knowing how to love.'

'You were very convincing,' Kate said carefully. She'd suffered terribly in the last few days, and this abrupt transformation was hard to take in. 'What changed, Noah? Did you remember that I can help you run Radnor, that I can be your business partner and look after Liv?'

A look of intense dismay came over him and he ran a distracted hand through his hair. 'I already knew that. Hell, Kate, this is not about *convenience*.'

She swallowed and took an instinctive step back, but the room was too small and she bumped into the wall. Noah came closer, blocking her escape, and his hands came to rest on the wall on either side of her, trapping her.

'Why—' she began, but her words were cut off as his head dipped towards her.

He kissed her skin just above her upper lip, softly, and with mesmerising tenderness, and then he kissed her again, moving his lips a fraction lower and increasing the pressure. Kate's entire body dissolved into a mass of warm sensations as his mouth travelled lower again, taking both her lips together, returning again to boldly tease them apart.

The Valentine's card slipped from her fingers and her hands rose to link behind his neck. He deepened the kiss. His hands came off the wall and they spanned her ribs, and her body began to burn with a painful, wonderful, hungry longing.

She knew she should stop this. Noah hadn't answered her questions. But her willpower had vanished with his first touch.

At the point where she knew her legs would give way beneath her, he stopped kissing and smiled down at her. 'That's about number seven on my list of reasons I love you, Kate Brodie. You have the loveliest, most inviting mouth.'

She felt a bright blush bloom in her cheeks. 'Number seven? You have six other reasons?'

'More than six.' He kissed her brow, her chin, her nose. He pressed warm kisses to her eyelids, her earlobes, her throat, and Kate thought she would actually swoon.

Noah's eyes grew serious. 'Do you remember our first kiss, when you were seventeen?'

'Of course. It changed my life.'

'Mine, too.' He touched her throat with his fingertips. 'You were so wonderfully, fearfully brave, Kate. So beautiful.'

'But I shocked you,' she said, pulling away from his touch. She couldn't think when he touched her, and she needed to *think*. She couldn't afford another mistake with this man.

'I wanted you so much, Kate.'

'You took off on your horse. You couldn't get away fast enough, and you stayed away till I'd left for England.'

'Because I was crazy about you, and I couldn't keep my promise to Angus unless I stayed well away from you.'

'What promise to Angus?'

'He was so worried about the responsibility of his sister's daughter from England. He made me swear that I wouldn't lay a hand on you.'

'Oh.' She could easily imagine how it had been—

Angus had been so estranged from her mother, and both of them had been influenced by their embittered parents.

'Is that why you never replied when I sent the Valentine card?'

'Yes. I know it was cruel to ignore you. I felt like a jerk, but I also knew I had to let you go, even though you would probably hate me for it. At least you could hate me, then forget me and move on.'

'It didn't work, Noah. I was still planning to come back to Australia, to find you and marry you. But you jumped the gun.'

He nodded, and his mouth twisted in a sad smile. 'With disastrous results.'

'While I've endured a string of unsatisfactory boyfriends.'

'Kate.' His fingers sifted her hair. 'I thought I'd lost you, darling girl.'

'I was sure I'd lost you.'

'I saw that bracelet and knew you'd gone and I wanted to die.'

He cradled her head against his big, broad shoulder. 'I kept seeing you crouched over a campfire with smoke in your eyes, or trying so hard to mount that damned horse. I remembered all the times you read a story to Liv when you were dead tired.' He touched her lips. 'I remembered your kisses, and I was terrified that I might never get to kiss you again.'

Against her ear, he said, 'I would have swum oceans. I would have travelled the entire globe till I found you, Kate. I love you. I want to make you happy. I really love you. I *know* I love you.'

All the time he'd been talking, she'd made his shirt damp with her tears.

'And, for the record, Liv loves you too. She's waiting for us back at Radnor.'

'So—so, are we talking long-term?' She *had* to ask. She had to be sure.

'Absolutely long-term.' He gave a little laugh, bubbling with happiness. 'You have no idea how good it feels to be able to say this with confidence. I love you. I'll do everything in my power to keep you happy.'

'You won't have to do much at all, Noah. If I'm with you, I'll be happy.' She remembered her fear of being a lonely little old lady in a nursing home, with nothing but faded, sad memories, and she shivered against him.

'You're cold, Kate. This dress is wet.'

She laughed softly, and then, as exhilaration welled and bubbled inside her, she laughed again and shot him a coy look. 'I suppose I should get out of it.'

'I suppose you should.' His smile was perfect. 'Why don't you let me help you?'

'So thoughtful of you to offer, sir.' Taking his hand, she led him into the adjoining room. She was walking on air, happier than she'd ever thought possible, but calm, too, buoyed by Noah's reassuring certainty.

Eyes shining, she turned to him. 'Do you think Uncle Angus knew this would happen to us when he changed his will?'

'I reckon he was counting on it.'

For a wistful moment they were lost in fond memories of the old man who'd meant so much to both of them.

Then, playfully, Kate looked about her. 'I'm afraid we have a minor problem. There's only one bedroom.'

Noah simply smiled, and he kissed her again as he began to untie the straps of her sundress.

EPILOGUE

KATE Carmody, in a chic black maternity dress—it had to be black and chic for London—clutched a glass of orange juice and tried to control her excited grin.

The boutique gallery in Knightsbridge was overflowing with journalists, editors from glossy magazines and even one or two television producers. Britain's top photographers and graphic artists rubbed shoulders with her family and friends, and all of them had come for one reason—the opening of her London exhibition.

The gallery's pristine white walls were lined with the glowing colours of the Australian Outback, and already an exciting number of red dots had been stuck beneath the prints.

The interest in Kate's photography had happened rather miraculously. A tiny exhibition at the Jindabilla Show had attracted excited attention, and as a result Kate had been asked to exhibit at the Royal Easter Show in Sydney. Then a visiting critic from the UK had been sufficiently ecstatic to set things rolling in London.

'But that must be an end to it,' Kate had told Noah. 'We'll have the show in London, and then I want to stay put at Radnor and extend our family.'

'More babies?' he'd chuckled. 'Aren't our two rowdy little boys enough?'

'I'd like two more.'

So the London exhibition had been carefully timed to be held after Noah and his team had mustered the Radnor cattle, and during Kate's middle trimester, the safest time for travelling.

And it seemed, already, that this showing would be a success. Kate had received enough praise to make her head swell. And that was *before* her girlfriends had started gushing about Noah.

'Cute', 'hot' and 'sexy' were high favourites among the adjectives the girls had used to describe her husband.

Well, of course, it was only to be expected, wasn't it? Noah looked extra gorgeous tonight in his formal evening clothes. The crisp white shirt highlighted his outdoorsy tan, and the lines of the suit showed off his lean, tough physique.

Kate felt a warm glow inside her as she watched him chatting politely to beaming strangers, charming them, no doubt, with his slow smile and quiet, laconic sense of humour.

Nearby was Liv, looking so grown up and tall now in an ankle-length white dress, and full of poise and self-importance as she offered trays of hors d'oeuvres to the guests.

Next year she would be leaving for boarding school and they would miss her terribly. But it was time for her to move on from the little school in Jindabilla, and she would do well. She was a bright student, and some of her friends were already at the same boarding school, including Brad Jameson's daughter, Meg.

'Now that is really something. Oh Nigel, I really love it. Let's buy it.'

Kate turned in surprise when she heard her mother's voice. She moved closer and said in little more than a whisper, 'You don't have to buy anything here, Mum. Just tell me what you'd like and I'll organise it.'

'Oh, darling, I love this one. I don't know why, there's just something about it that draws me.'

Kate stared at her mother's choice in surprise. She and Nigel had been to Radnor on several occasions now, and they'd enjoyed themselves tremendously each time. But this was a photo Kate had taken long ago, when she'd first arrived for Angus's funeral.

It showed part of the front steps and a deep-pink frangipani tree glowing in the sunlight, and then a slice across the veranda past the timber-and-canvas chair to the open front door.

'See that old hat and the bridle hanging beside the door?' Kate said, pointing.

'Yes. They're part of the reason I like this picture. I expect someone to walk out that door, grab that hat and jump on a horse.'

'It was Angus's hat, Mum. That's just how he left it.'

Her mother smiled, but her eyes sparkled too brightly, and Kate slipped an arm around her shoulders and hugged her.

'If only he knew how well everything's turned out,' her mother said shakily. 'If only he could see how happy you and Noah are. And he would have loved your dear little Angus and Fred.'

'I'm sure he knew everything would be fine, Mum.' Kate gave her mother's shoulders another squeeze. 'He knew when he changed his will.'

Kate looked across the room and saw Noah watching them. He smiled at her, a smile so full of warmth and love it started a slow meltdown inside her.

Noah excused himself and began to make his way through the crowd towards her. Watching him, Kate felt as fluttery and in love as she had all those years ago when she'd behaved so rashly at the age of seventeen.

Now she was in her thirties and sensible, a married woman, a mother, and an artist who'd attracted international respect. And this was an occasion that called for decorum, but, as she took two steps towards her husband, he opened his arms, and, throwing caution to the wind, she kissed him passionately in front of all these respectable people.

* * * * *

*Celebrate 60 years of pure reading pleasure
with Harlequin®!*
*Silhouette® Romantic Suspense is celebrating with
the glamour-filled, adrenaline-charged series
LOVE IN 60 SECONDS starting in April 2009.
Six stories that promise to bring the glitz of
Las Vegas, the danger of revenge, the mystery
of a missing diamond, family scandals and
ripped-from-the-headlines intrigue.
Get your heart racing as love happens
in sixty seconds!*

*Enjoy a sneak peek of
USA TODAY bestselling author Marie Ferrarella's
THE HEIRESS'S 2-WEEK AFFAIR
Available April 2009
from Silhouette® Romantic Suspense.*

Eight years ago Matt Shaffer had vanished out of Natalie Rothchild's life, leaving behind a one-line note tucked under a pillow that had grown cold: *I'm sorry, but this just isn't going to work.*

That was it. No explanation, no real indication of remorse. The note had been as clinical and compassionless as an eviction notice, which, in effect, it had been, Natalie thought as she navigated through the morning traffic. Matt had written the note to evict her from his life.

She'd spent the next two weeks crying, breaking down without warning as she walked down the street, or as she sat staring at a meal she couldn't bring herself to eat.

Candace, she remembered with a bittersweet pang, had tried to get her to go clubbing in order to get her to forget about Matt.

She'd turned her twin down, but she did get her act together. If Matt didn't think enough of their relationship to try to contact her, to try to make her understand why he'd changed so radically from lover to stranger, then to hell with him. He was dead to her, she resolved. And he'd remained that way.

Until twenty minutes ago.

The adrenaline in her veins kept mounting.

Natalie focused on her driving. Vegas in the daylight wasn't nearly as alluring, as magical and glitzy as it was after dark. Like an aging woman best seen in soft lighting, Vegas's imperfections were all visible in the daylight. Natalie supposed that was why people like her sister didn't like to get up until noon. They lived for the night.

Except that Candace could no longer do that.

The thought brought a fresh, sharp ache with it.

"Damn it, Candy, what a waste," Natalie murmured under her breath.

She pulled up before the Janus casino. One of the three valets currently on duty came to life and made a beeline for her vehicle.

"Welcome to the Janus," the young attendant said cheerfully as he opened her door with a flourish.

"We'll see," she replied solemnly.

As he pulled away with her car, Natalie looked up at the casino's logo. Janus was the Roman god with two faces, one pointed toward the past, the other facing the future. It struck her as rather ironic, given what she was doing here, seeking out someone from her past in order to get answers so that the future could be settled.

The moment she entered the casino, the Vegas phenomena took hold. It was like stepping into a world where time did not matter or even make an appearance. There was only a sense of "now."

Because in Natalie's experience she'd discovered that bartenders knew the inner workings of any establishment they worked for better than anyone else, she made her way to the first bar she saw within the casino.

The bartender in attendance was a gregarious man in his early forties. He had a quick, sexy smile, which was probably one of the main reasons he'd been hired. His name tag identified him as Kevin.

Moving to her end of the bar, Kevin asked, "What'll it be, pretty lady?"

"Information." She saw a dubious look cross his brow. To counter that, she took out her badge. Granted she wasn't here in an official capacity, but Kevin didn't need to know that. "Were you on duty last night?"

Kevin began to wipe the gleaming black surface of the bar. "You mean during the gala?"

"Yes."

The smile gracing his lips was a satisfied one. Last night had obviously been profitable for him, she judged. "I caught an extra shift."

She took out Candace's photograph and carefully placed it on the bar. "Did you happen to see this woman there?"

The bartender glanced at the picture. Mild interest turned to recognition. "You mean Candace Rothchild? Yeah, she was here, loud and brassy as always. But not for long," he added, looking rather disappointed. There was always a circus when Candace was around, Natalie thought. "She and the boss had at it and then he had our head of security escort her out."

She latched onto the first part of his statement. "They argued? About what?"

He shook his head. "Couldn't tell you. Too far away for anything but body language," he confessed.

"And the head of security?" she asked.

"He got her to leave."

She leaned in over the bar. "Tell me about him."

"Don't know much," the bartender admitted. "Just that his name's Matt Shaffer. Boss flew him in from L.A., where he was head of security for Montgomery Enterprises."

There was no avoiding it, she thought darkly. She was going to have to talk to Matt. The thought left her cold. "Do you know where I can find him right now?"

Kevin glanced at his watch. "He should be in his office. On the second floor, toward the rear." He gave her the numbers of the rooms where the monitors that kept watch over the casino guests as they tried their luck against the house were located.

Taking out a twenty, she placed it on the bar. "Thanks for your help."

Kevin slipped the bill into his vest pocket. "Any time, lovely lady," he called after her. "Any time."

She debated going up the stairs, then decided on the elevator. The car that took her up to the second floor was empty. Natalie stepped out of the elevator, looked around to get her bearings and then walked toward the rear of the floor.

"Into the Valley of Death rode the six hundred," she silently recited, digging deep for a line from a poem by Tennyson. Wrapping her hand around a brass handle, she opened one of the glass doors and walked in.

The woman whose desk was closest to the door looked up. "You can't come in here. This is a restricted area."

Natalie already had her ID in her hand and held it up. "I'm looking for Matt Shaffer," she told the woman.

God, even saying his name made her mouth go dry. She was supposed to be over him, to have moved on with her life. What happened?

The woman began to answer her. "He's—"

"Right here."

The deep voice came from behind her. Natalie felt every single nerve ending go on tactical alert at the same moment that all the hairs at the back of her neck stood up. Eight years had passed, but she would have recognized his voice anywhere.

*****

Why did Matt Shaffer leave
heiress-turned-cop Natalie Rothchild?
What does he know about the death of
Natalie's twin sister?
Come and meet these two reunited lovers
and learn the secrets of the Rothchild family in
THE HEIRESS'S 2-WEEK AFFAIR
by USA TODAY bestselling author
Marie Ferrarella.
The first book in Silhouette® Romantic Suspense's
wildly romantic new continuity,
LOVE IN 60 SECONDS!
Available April 2009.

REQUEST YOUR FREE BOOKS!
2 FREE NOVELS PLUS 2
FREE GIFTS!

HARLEQUIN ROMANCE

From the Heart, For the Heart

YES! Please send me 2 FREE Harlequin Romance® novels and my 2 FREE gifts (gifts are worth about $10). After receiving them, if I don't wish to receive any more books, I can return the shipping statement marked "cancel". If I don't cancel, I will receive 4 brand-new novels every month and be billed just $3.32 per book in the U.S. or $3.80 per book in Canada, plus 25¢ shipping and handling per book and applicable taxes, if any*. That's a savings of over 15% off the cover price! I understand that accepting the 2 free books and gifts places me under no obligation to buy anything. I can always return a shipment and cancel at any time. Even if I never buy another book, the two free books and gifts are mine to keep forever.

114 HDN ERQW 314 HDN ERQ9

Name	(PLEASE PRINT)	
Address		Apt. #
City	State/Prov.	Zip/Postal Code

Signature (if under 18, a parent or guardian must sign)

Mail to the Harlequin Reader Service:
IN U.S.A.: P.O. Box 1867, Buffalo, NY 14240-1867
IN CANADA: P.O. Box 609, Fort Erie, Ontario L2A 5X3

Not valid to current subscribers of Harlequin Romance books.

Want to try two free books from another line?
Call 1-800-873-8635 or visit www.morefreebooks.com.

* Terms and prices subject to change without notice. N.Y. residents add applicable sales tax. Canadian residents will be charged applicable provincial taxes and GST. Offer not valid in Quebec. This offer is limited to one order per household. All orders subject to approval. Credit or debit balances in a customer's account(s) may be offset by any other outstanding balance owed by or to the customer. Please allow 4 to 6 weeks for delivery. Offer available while quantities last.

Your Privacy: Harlequin Books is committed to protecting your privacy. Our Privacy Policy is available online at www.eHarlequin.com or upon request from the Reader Service. From time to time we make our lists of customers available to reputable third parties who may have a product or service of interest to you. If you would prefer we not share your name and address, please check here. ☐

HR08R